Accidentally Under Your Tree

GRAND RIDGE CHRISTMAS

MARTY VEE

Contents

One

Lizzy

SEVEN NIGHTS BEFORE CHRISTMAS

Me: The man sitting next to me has the most beautiful hands.

Shay: LOL You and your hand obsession.

Me: No, these are exceptional. They're like Hozier meets Henry Cavill.

Shay: Only you could name-drop hands you find sexy.

Me: Lots of people have a thing for hands.

Shay: Why is a hand fetish more socially acceptable than a foot fetish?

Me: IDK. I don't make the rules, but even you would be attracted to these hands.

Shay: Oh no, I'm a wrist girl. Like a slut.

I surprised myself with a squeaky-toy-like laugh, startling the middle-aged woman to my right, and the hot man attached to the artistic hands to my left. Wide palms with long, calloused fingers—hands that looked like they could build something more complicated than Ikea furniture. It'd shock me if they hadn't held sandpaper this week.

I had a type. And it was hands.

"Sorry," I whispered to the two strangers.

The woman had already gone back to sipping her glass of wine and playing a word game on her phone.

But the man gave me a shy, lopsided grin. My stomach flipped with the same sudden panic I'd felt a few hours ago, when my boot slipped on the ice outside of the hotel door. I recovered from the near fall more gracefully than I did from his mossy green eyes.

Slurping more air than drink, I sucked my vodka cranberry through the straw. The gurgling was probably quieter than it seemed in my head.

Behind us, people laughed at tables covered with plates and glasses. In the dim golden lighting, a pianist played jazzy Christmas carols. I pretended to watch the young woman to gain distance between me and the handsome man and his cozy cable-knit sweater draping over his shoulders—wide...broad shoulders.

When I was sure his attention had returned to his phone, I snatched up mine again.

> Me: Don't make me laugh!

Shay: I can't just turn off this God-given-wit.

> Me: He just looked at me! And you know I hate when people notice me!

Shay: *eye roll emoji* Is the rest of him hot?

> Me: *fire emoji*

Shay: Is there a wedding ring on those beautiful fingers?

> Me: No.

Shay: Then I'm gonna need you to get over your people weirdness.

> Me: You can't make me.

Shay: You're the one who could have a future date with those hands…

The churning of my stomach clearly stated that I was not "over my people weirdness." And it wasn't *people* I struggled with. I did great when I knew someone. Not exactly a social butterfly like my sister, but Shay was just as introverted as me. She just had an easier time meeting people.

The anxiety of someone *new*…that was a bit much. I wiped my clammy hands on my pant leg.

Sure, my ex and I had broken up almost ten months before, and I'd emotionally checked out of the relationship long before it ended. And apparently, so had he.

But talk to a stranger? No, thank you.

Even if Shay pissed me right off, she kinda had a point. Not because of the man sitting next to me, but because of the career I was trying to build. Management consulting wasn't a perfect match for my social-anxiety-ridden ass. But I was good at it. And all the socializing aside, I really liked it. I was also undercharging my clients—desperate times, desperate measures. Ten and a half months into owning my firm, and I'd just completed my first referral job. Progress.

I was staying an extra night in the city before heading home. Home, to my parents' house. It was bound to be crazy for the next week leading into Christmas, with my mom's natural enthusiasm and my sister bringing a new man home.

I missed having my quiet apartment, filled with my favorite orange and cinnamon scented candles and knit blanket. It sucked living in the same bedroom I once imagined marrying JC from *NSYNC in, but it was free.

Thanks, Mom and Dad.

Again, desperate times.

I chased an ice cube around my empty glass with the thin plastic straw. When the bartender asked if I'd like another, I forced a polite smile and shook my head.

I was a little buzzed, but I wasn't feeling bad. It was probably the right time to go up to my room.

Wind whipped wet snow against the window.

My knees were a stiff as I stood. My butt numbed from the bar stool. It took me a second to balance.

That was when the power went out.

The whir of machines silenced. The lights turned off all at once.

The storm thrashed against the building.

My hand shot out and grabbed the first solid object I could find in the nearly pitch black. The solid object reached back and held my waist.

There were a few clatter notes from the piano before it fell silent. The dining area filled with the screams and gasps of people, surprised by the sudden reach of the storm. It'd snapped its fingers and broken our bubble, reminding us that our security was only as thick as the walls.

The clean, comforting smell of soap filled my nose.

Over the beating of my heart and the nervous murmurs around me, a gentle voice rumbled up the skin of my neck. It cast goosebumps down my arms and seeped into my sternum—a warm whispered, "I've got you."

Two

Will

SEVEN NIGHTS BEFORE CHRISTMAS

I waited for her grip to loosen on my shoulder. I'd let go as soon as she did. Her profile lit in the dimness; the very tips of her eyelashes captured the light like fairy dust. But I couldn't see her eyes, just the soft parting of her lips. The startled rise and fall of her chest. She was close enough to identify the citrus scent I'd caught traces of all night.

Her ribs expanded into my palm.

She tightened her grip, and mine flexed in response—sinking into the soft flesh of her waist.

"The backup lights will kick on," I said. They should have turned on already. "It'll be okay."

She nodded in jerky movements. "Right."

Turning her neck, she faced me. The light drawing new lines—the curve of her cheek, wisps of hair that had escaped her ponytail.

Emergency lights illuminated at the bottom of every exit sign. I could make out her wide eyes were some shade of brown. It was only fair that I note her eyes, when I'd already taken in the way her thighs filled out her professional looking pants... And the way she filled out the cardigan sweater thing she was wearing. When she'd glared back at me a few minutes before, it'd almost been a relief. Rose would kill me if I were caught flirting with some stranger at a hotel bar—it was a nice hotel, but just the phrase was seedy enough.

Not that people usually recognized me outside of a home improvement store.

She and I had an agreement. It wouldn't be long before we could go back to normal.

The stranger tore her hand away as if she'd been holding a venomous snake and not my shoulder.

"S-s-sorry," she stammered. "So sorry."

I lowered my arm to rest on my thigh, flexing my hand between my knees. "No problem. Are you okay—"

"I'm fine," she cut me off.

"Okay."

She lowered back to her stool as if sinking into unchartered territory, her shoulders tight and lifted toward her ears. To our left, the bartender frantically wrote down room numbers from diners demanding to leave.

"Should I go up to my room?" she asked.

I shrugged. "I was wondering the same thing."

Somehow, she drew even tighter. "I know I said that out loud, but I wasn't actually asking you."

Holding up my hand in unspoken apology, I said, "Understood."

Over the chaos swirling around us, she let out a slow exhale between her pursed lips. Her hands folded on her lap. She held so still she could have been the sculpture of an unsure woman in the 21st century.

I could practically hear Rose snickering in my head, *"Billiam, you are a damn fool."*

Imaginary Rose made a brilliant point. This strange woman had only given me signals to leave her alone, and I would, but goddamn if it didn't make her sexier.

"You like them so prickly, you're gonna fall in love with a cactus."

I rolled my eyes, even if I was actually irritated with myself and not imaginary Rose.

"So, what are you going to do?" the hot cactus lady asked.

Folding my arms on the bar top, I settled in. "I'm gonna sit here for a while." I jerked my head toward the people lined up to talk to the bartender. "Let that mess calm down."

Meeting the woman's eyes straight on, I continued, "I'm sure the stairway is even worse with people coming down, people going up. I have ten flights to climb, and I'm not looking forward to it."

"That's a lot of stairs."

"It is. So, I'll wait right here. Maybe the power will come on and stay on for a little while and I can take the elevator."

"That's not a bad plan." She nodded, looking straight ahead before her eyes widened. "Our room keys. Will our room keys even work?"

She paused opening the browser app on her phone, when I answered, "Hotel locks are on a battery powered system. Your key should work fine."

Blinking, she locked her phone screen and put her full, surly focus on me. "How do you know that?"

"I'm a general contractor. I've done some hotel work."

"I guess I'll trust you then."

"You can look it up. I don't mind."

"You have calloused hands."

I coughed a laugh, and my jaw tightened. I'd been reduced to "working class" before. It was true, but it still felt condescending. With a bit more bite in my tone than I expected, I replied, "Must have missed my manicure this week."

"I didn't mean to insult you."

"You know, not everyone with calloused hands could answer that question."

"I do. I...I just noticed, and so when you said what you do, it was evidence that you're telling the truth."

"Are you a lawyer?"

A crease formed between her light brown eyebrows. "No, I'm a consultant."

"What kind of consultant?"

"Management. I assess systems and make them more efficient to increase productivity and profit."

"So, you're perceptive?"

The whisper of a smile tugged at one corner of her mouth, hinting at a dimple. "Yeah." Twirling her stud earring, she chewed on her lip. "How recently have you held sandpaper?"

This time my laugh wasn't sardonic. "Uh...it wasn't for work, but...Tuesday or Wednesday."

The blood pumped a little hotter through my veins at her pleased little grin.

"I knew it." Her voice was buttery, smooth.

A smile spread across my face. I didn't know what she meant, but it was safe to assume she'd noticed me, too.

"I'm Will."

"Lizzy."

Three

Lizzy

SIX NIGHTS BEFORE CHRISTMAS

"Holy shit." Mom cried with a hand to her chest. "I didn't know you were home."

"Sorry," I said. "I got home a couple of hours ago. I was in the basement to get some work done."

When I'd arrived home, chatting with my parents was something I wanted to avoid. Not after the night I'd had.

Moving back into my childhood home felt like the end of my old life. The one where I was an adult. Capable of coming and going as I pleased. I had my privacy. Although my parents weren't meddlers, they were invested. They liked to know...*everything*.

I just wanted to be left alone.

"How was the trip?" she asked.

"Good."

I sat at the kitchen island. Its quartz top was cold under my forearms. The white surface was clean and shiny. Outside the window over the sink, the trees' shadows lengthened—it was only midafternoon, but already the sun was beginning to set.

Mom flitted from the stand mixer to the fridge, her silver bob bouncing with each step. We made small talk about my past few days. I omitted everything about last night except the storm. She'd gotten the scoop on some of the competitors for the Christmas tree decorating contest.

"They don't stand a chance. Your sister and I have come up with the most incredible design." She turned her back to me opening the oven. The comforting, mouth-watering scent of Shepard's pie wafted into the kitchen. "You'll still help us, right?"

By "help" she meant carry things.

"Planning on it."

"Your sister should be here in a few hours. I'm so excited. Both my girls under the same roof." Her blue eyes were bright with optimism. Leave it to my mom to have faith that this year her daughters would make up. Like every year for the past eight, I was positive she'd be disappointed. I would be too.

My stomach twisted with anxiety. Seeing my twin and only sibling brought complicated emotions.

"Is it intimidating that she's bringing her new boyfriend? It's been years since you've celebrated Christmas without Brian."

"Mom, I'm fine being single. I'm more embarrassed I had to move back home."

"Oh, that's nothing to be embarrassed of."

"You're right...why on earth would I feel like a loser for that?"

"You're not a loser. You're getting back on your feet." With each word, she sounded more patient, meaning she was getting more irritated.

"Thanks, Mom. It's all better now." It was one snark too far.

"Young lady." Mom put a hand on her narrow hip. Speaking with the exact tone she used to scold me when I was nine, she said, "I will not have you talking badly about yourself. You are wonderful, and talented, and we don't mope around."

Back to feeling like a child.

"The way I feel is valid." I'd made this point before—it was not well received then either.

"It's nonsense. Lots of people move back in with their parents."

"And they feel like shit about it."

"What's there to feel like shit about? So, what if people judge you? Who cares?"

I sighed. As if she wasn't just as concerned with what people thought of her. I'd seen the way she changed the subject when anyone mentioned that I was living with them now, she'd redirect the conversation to my business.

"Okay, Mom." Taking a step backward, I moved toward the hallway. "I'm gonna go get cleaned up."

"I'll let you know when your sister's here."

"You don't have to. We'll see each other when we see each other."

Disappointment ebbed off my mom like radiation—I couldn't physically feel it, but I knew it was there. She shook her head. Her lips pinched, as if holding back her thoughts.

I closed my bedroom door behind me. The room was painted the same color as when I was a kid. Mom had been talking about redecorating it about a month before I moved back. Maybe it wouldn't feel so much like regression if she had, but I couldn't justify the cost and energy of painting when my stay here was temporary.

At least my desk looked like a well-organized adult used it. My color-coded stationary, pens, and post-it notes in their place. If there was anything I liked spending my money on the most, it was office supplies.

I was unsure about how long it would take me to get out of here. My business was doing fairly well for its first year. By this time next year, *maybe* I could have my own place.

I shot a text to Shay asking about her day, then threw my phone on my vanilla-colored knitted blanket. Almost instantly, a return message arrived. I finished deciding on a cozy sweater and joggers from my dresser before reading what she'd said.

> Shay: Fine. Work was slow today. I don't know whether to curse your parents for making me work this week or thank them. I've gotten so much reading done.

> Me: I wish I could get paid to read.

> Shay: It's pretty good. The phone has rung like three times since Monday. Anyway, it's not like my house is peaceful right now, with Lawrence working on my fireplace.

She sent a photo of the progress, including her brother, Lawrence, glaring at the camera. He wasn't offended by his picture being taken, that was just his face.

The phone buzzed again as I changed from one leisure outfit to a slightly more presentable, possibly even stylish, leisure outfit. Looking casual and unaffected at being face-to-face with my sister while meeting her new boyfriend and looking like I cared too much, was a fine line to walk.

The boyfriend that was, apparently, well loved by her fans. His fans too.

I didn't watch their little YouTube show, so I wouldn't know.

Everyone in town watched it, though. And they all liked to talk. I just nodded my head and agreed. Let them assume I knew what they were talking about. The boundaries I drew to avoid the pain of watching my sister's life and not being a part of it were my concern, not theirs.

While pulling the scrunchy out of my hair, I unlocked my phone to read Shay's text.

Shay: Are they there yet?

Me: Mom said they will be in a couple of hours.

Shay: Hopefully, her bringing a man will make this visit less dramatic. I cannot take another holiday of Lawrence, all heartbroken and depressed.

Me: One can only hope.

I finished the French braid that ended at my shoulders, with only a few of my curls escaping around my temples. Stepping into the hallway, I smiled a greeting to my dad sitting behind the desk in the study. Through the study's other entrance, I saw my mom considering three little gold decorative snowmen displayed on the end table. She pinched one of the hats and turned it forty-five degrees.

When she noticed me watching her, she looked up with the tilt of her lips.

"Is it just right now?" Dad asked, still typing in a slow, deliberate cadence.

"I think so."

"Looks good, Mom."

"Thanks, Lizzy."

Just like that, the argument in the kitchen would go unresolved until the next time we repeated the pattern.

I looked down at my phone as a new message came through, only a little disappointed that it was from Shay and not Will. He hadn't said he would text me today, but I hoped he would.

Why hadn't I gotten his number?

Shay: You stopped texting last night. What happened?

Me: ...This is not the proper medium for this conversation.

Shay: NO SHIT! Give me something, don't leave me in suspense.

I paused typing out a quick response, when Mom opened the front door, and my sister walked through. Her dark blue wool coat tailored perfectly to her petite frame, and matched her, and mom's, eyes. Her smile was so bright it created its own light source. She looked healthy and happy. For that, I was grateful.

"Rosebud!" Mom cried out.

So much for a couple of hours.

They hugged each other tight.

"Is Rosie home?" Dad stood, his office chair rolling against the bookshelf behind him.

Rose's boyfriend stepped just inside the door. The first thing I noticed about him was his hands. He carried the suitcase with strong, square fingers. His knuckles were almost as wide as the plastic handle. Capable hands.

Blood rushed from my head, and I blinked, suddenly dizzy.

No way.

But I knew the truth even before I took in the scruff on his sharp jaw. Or the lines bracketing his warm smile. Or his dark eyelashes surrounding his moss green eyes.

Rat. Bastard.

Four

Will

SIX NIGHTS BEFORE CHRISTMAS

I shifted the rental car into park outside of a scenic little brick ranch. Icicles clung from the gutters on either side of the porch. A wreath of what looked like real pine boughs hung on the front door. It was adorable.

And I was going to go inside of this adorable house and lie to its occupants.

I turned to Rose sitting in the passenger seat. "We aren't going to have to kiss, are we?"

Her face twisted in disgust. "Why?"

Despite the minor blow to my ego, it was a comfort that she and I agreed.

"To prove our relationship." I shrugged.

Her snort vaguely reminded me of Lizzy from the hotel bar, but then...I'd been thinking about Lizzy a lot over the past few hours.

The two women couldn't be more different, especially considering the dynamic chemistry I'd had with Lizzy. And although Rose was beautiful with her blue eyes and angular face, she and I had only ever been just friends.

She shook her head. "No, Billiam, you sweet, sweet boy. They're not going to make us kiss to prove our relationship. My family does not want to see that. Why would we have to prove anything?"

I raised one eyebrow in her direction.

She smiled at me in a *aren't you adorable* sort of way—that was usually endearing, but I currently hated. "If you're going to look guilty, then they will know something is up."

Drumming my fingers on the steering wheel, I walked backward in my memory, wondering how I got from point A to point HERE.

"Just be your normal self and your charm'll dazzle them." She sounded less confident with every word, a fault in the facade.

"It, you know, made so much sense when we decided to do this—"

"Yeah," she agreed, showing a bit more of the nerves we obviously shared.

"—but now..."

"We're going to convince my family that we're in a relationship."

I pinched my lips between my teeth and nodded.

She swallowed. "But I don't think it'll matter as much as it feels like it does right now."

The queasy twist in my gut didn't believe her.

"It's not like they'll be heartbroken when we tell them we broke up. Especially since we're still going to be friends afterward and all of that."

"Yup."

"It's almost like if you and I were in an actual relationship, but we weren't in a very physical phase. We're in the like comfortable-silence-pal-ing around part. Right?"

She was convincing herself as much as she was convincing me, but it was working. The tightness in my chest loosened slightly.

"That's a good point."

"And technically," she continued, her voice brightening as she spoke, "we are exclusive for the next couple of weeks. You're not gonna go on a date, and neither am I, and everything's cool, you know?"

When she put it that way, I kinda wanted to come clean about the way I'd spent my time last night, but our agreement didn't start until she picked me up from the hotel. So, I wasn't technically in the *wrong*.

"That's a very good point." The unease in my stomach relaxed. "It's not like your parents are gonna fall head over heels for me in a week."

"According to the network, they fit your target audience."

My face split with a grin. "The network."

The one that had rejected turning our YouTube channel into a show for their streaming service. But even the rejection had been a little thrilling.

"It has such a ring to it." She smiled back, her eyes sparkling.

When Elise, our agent, approached us to sell *Will it Bloom Renovations* to a streaming service, we'd almost dismissed the possibility. Then decided to go for it. Why not, right?

Rose and I were out of our depth, but Elise knew more about all of this than we did. She'd suggested we appear more unified, based on the input from the rejecting network. I didn't know if pretending to date was what she had in mind. Our fanbase seemed happy about it. The announcement had been flooded with comments about Rose and me being a cute couple.

According to our social media profiles, we were "trying it out." A perfect place to back track without creating too much drama. There weren't a ton of people paying attention, anyway. We weren't a huge show, even in YouTube standards.

It'd only be for a couple of weeks before returning to normal.

Hopefully, Lizzy would still be interested in hearing from me by then. I really wished meeting her hadn't timed so poorly with this little farce. I hadn't called or messaged her yet. But the temptation was real.

She didn't seem like she could fall into such a hair-brained idea. Rose and I might not have gone this far if Rose hadn't complained about inevitably seeing her ex-boyfriend when she went home for Christmas.

"I swear," she'd whined, "fucking him is detrimental to my health, but I cannot stop myself. I need a goddamn babysitter."

It was unclear how we'd gone from that comment to texting her parents that I'd be joining her. Like most of our choices, the decision happened quickly and without a lot of forethought. Her flight was fully booked, so I'd opted to fly in a night earlier.

Now we were in her parents' driveway as the sky turned dark purple, bright pink, and gold.

A pine tree strung with lights and stockings hung on the mantle, created a perfect Christmas scene through the bay window.

If I had gone to my mom or dad's, the view would be different. Neither of my parents did much for the holidays. Luckily, neither of them was exceptionally upset that I would miss this year. They were disappointed, but they just understood.

Or they thought they did. Actually, I had lied through my teeth about a budding relationship between me and Rose.

I scraped my palm across my jaw. "What about your sister?"

Rose's shoulders tightened like they usually did when someone mentioned her twin. "What about Anne?"

"Is she gonna believe us?"

Rose scoffed. "Anne won't care. She'll avoid us all week, anyway. She's like a temperamental house cat with new people. She might even hiss at you."

Snorting, I joked, "If she's that bad, I'm doomed to fall in love with her."

"Don't you dare!" Rose shifted in her seat, leaning her back against the passenger door. A mixture of terror and outrage filled her blue eyes.

"I won't."

Despite the speed that I fell for Lizzy, I didn't become infatuated with every grumpy woman I met.

"God." Rose groaned. "I didn't even think about that. What a nightmare."

"I was just kidding."

She sighed, resting her head on the window behind her. "I'm more anxious than I thought I would be."

My comforting smile felt tight at the edges, but it was my turn to set her at ease. "It'll be okay. We'll be pretty much the same. I just might hold your hand sometimes."

"I can survive handholding."

"It's just a couple of weeks."

She sat up straight, her shoulders squared. "Just a couple of weeks. Come here, let's do a pic for Internet people."

Holding her phone at arm's length, she put her other elbow behind her on the center council. I leaned forward, placing my chin near her shoulder. We smiled at the camera, both of us looking a little unsure.

"Um...maybe look at me out of the corner of your eye or something," she suggested.

"I can do that."

"Nope. That's not good."

"Just smile at the camera?"

"Yeah, we'll try other things later."

She typed out a little caption, then posted the image to the show's stories.

I pushed my door open, and the frigid wind hit my face.

"It is so goddamn cold up here!" Rose grumbled, filing out of the car as well. "I'm making them come to me next year."

"Get inside. I'll grab the bags."

"Aren't you a good little boyfriend?" She took quick steps to the front door.

Her comment didn't sit right. I'd probably get more used to it. This strange title that didn't make any sense in our friendship.

"Sure am." I hit the fob to open the trunk. With her full-size suitcase in one hand and my slightly smaller one in the other, I followed her to the porch as the door swung open.

"Rosebud!" a middle-aged woman exclaimed. Her short silver hair curled toward her jaw. Her smile reminded me so much of Rose, it felt like I already knew her.

"Hi Momma."

Pulling her daughter into a hug, the two women hurried through the doorway, making room for me to walk through.

"I'm so glad you're here!" her mom exclaimed.

I set the luggage on the tile floor and closed the door. The white-pink walls were a bold choice, but it worked with the emerald green sofa and gold accents throughout the room. It wasn't a room for everyone's taste. Based on what Rose had said about learning design elements from her mom, it was intentional and obviously what her mom wanted.

"Is Rosie home?" A man's gruff voice called from an adjoining room.

"She is!" Her mom answered, still holding her daughter tight.

A large man walked through an archway to the left, and I glimpsed a woman darting down the hallway. A door closed directly after. She moved quickly, just a flash of soft fabric and brown hair.

My stomach flipped. My heart jumped. My throat grew tight. I had to remind myself that just because I wanted to see Lizzy again—it didn't mean she was here. It was Anne, Rose's sister, who apparently actually was like a house cat and scurrying away instead of meeting me.

Their parents, Jim, and Kelly passed out hugs and welcomes. Their joy at having Rose home was infectious. In only a matter of minutes, I had a mug of coffee in my hand and the promise of Shepard's pie for dinner.

It was a whirlwind of excitement until it came to a screeching halt. The blood drained from my face. My vision darkened around the edges. Everyone suddenly sounded as if they were underwater—or I guess, I would be the one underwater.

Above the fireplace mantle were photos of the family. The largest one was from when Rose and Anne must have been in high school. There was hardly any resemblance between the two girls. Where Rose took after her mom, Anne looked like her dad.

It was a smaller, more recent photo that stopped my heart.

I had to remind myself to breathe.

I startled when Jim—surprisingly silent for how big he was—stood next to me. "Isn't that a pretty picture?"

I choked out a sort of hum.

"That was at my niece's wedding this summer." He took a sip from his coffee, looking over his shoulder. "Lizzy's around here somewhere."

My mouth was too dry. I didn't know how I could form words. "I thought she was Anne."

"Some people still call her Anne. We named the girls' Rose and Lisianthus after our mom's favorite flowers. She was always Lizzy to me."

Fuuuuuuck.

Five

Lizzy

SIX NIGHTS BEFORE CHRISTMAS

"That rat bastard," Shay hissed.

I flicked my eyes from side to side, ensuring the other patrons of Benji's Place couldn't overhear. The local bar was quiet even for a Thursday evening.

Thank God.

I didn't want any of the town gossips—and there were many—getting a whisper of my situation.

When I'd texted Shay to get me, I'd imagined we'd go back to her place. I pictured the two of us on her sofa as I spilled my guts and drank away my sorrows. We'd watch *New Girl* for the hundredth time and eat chicken wings and jalapeño poppers from her freezer. I might even let my guard down enough to cry.

It wasn't until she turned toward town instead of her house that I remembered her older brother, Rose's ex boyfriend, Lawrence, was fixing something at Shay's house.

And since my house was ground zero to the future worst moment of my life, we couldn't stay there.

Which brought us to Benji's Place so at least I could have a stiff drink while I lamented. None of the tables neighboring our booths were occupied. That didn't stop my nerves.

Strands of white lights and garlands were strung along the ceiling and down the beams on each end of the bar. They reflected off the polished wood surfaces. A mix of classic and current Christmas music played from the speakers. It could have been homey if I wasn't in the shittiest mood.

Ben, the bar's owner, would probably forgive me if I ran around tearing down lights and screaming like Veruca Salt. Although the concept of throwing a fit was appealing, facing more consequences than the ones stacked in front of me...I'd pass.

Shocked silence washed over Shay and myself after I'd finished the story. The details I was looking forward to telling her had become sharped edged and scraped painfully on my throat now that I knew. Now that I wasn't sharing the details of a whirlwind budding infatuation, but a sordid affair. She soaked up the depressing absurdity in a quiet outrage. While I sat drenched in the inevitable ramifications of my actions.

My limbs and heart were too heavy. It felt like I was sinking.

I lifted my drink to my lips, but the whiskey mixed with apple and cinnamon turned my stomach and I set it back down. "Please say something."

"About *this*?" Shay's brown eyes widened. "I'm still processing."

"No, something else. Anything else."

She blew out a heavy sigh, puffing her cheeks. "Um...I can't think."

"Yeah..."

After a few beats, she said, "I posted a job to hire a new carpenter for the shop."

"Cool. Cool..."

Shay had worked at my parent's home renovation business since she graduated from college. She was slowly stepping into the role of business manager as her brother took over more project managing. Relinquishing control was hard for Mom and Dad, but they didn't want to work forever.

The only two people they *might* trust more with the company was me and Rose, and there was no way that was going to happen.

My phone buzzed. Our eyes snapped to it on the tabletop. A text from an unsaved number lit up by screen, ***Please let me explain.***

The proverbial twist of the knife in my chest. On my shoulder, his teeth marks burned.

"Is that him?" Shay demanded.

I shook my head and shrugged.

She narrowed her dark brown eyes at the phone before it went black again. "Explain what, motherfucker?"

I clenched my jaw, overwhelmed by the ferocity of my thoughts and disgust. How the hell had I been so naïve? I wanted to blame Will for everything, but I'd been the one to let my guard down. I was the one who had committed a terrible betrayal—one that I'd have to tell Rose about. She was going to hate me even more than she already did.

I was to blame for getting carried away by blind hope.

It was laughable the high I'd woken up on. Wrapped in white hotel sheets, I'd stretched with a wide smile on my face. My very first thought was of Will. It felt good to be noticed. Seen. Wanted.

I'd practically danced from room to room like a Disney Princess fallen in love with prince charming.

My phone buzzed again.

"That jackass," I mumbled through my clenched teeth.

"Block his number," Shay ordered.

"How?" I asked.

"I don't know. I'll google it."

Crossing my arms, I slouched back in my booth and tried to ignore the texts coming through. Each one was a fresh layer of hell. I flipped the phone screen side down. Phrases like *I'm sorry* and *not real*, did nothing for my mental state.

Yeah, I know it was all bullshit. I blinked back the moisture stinging my eyes.

"Okay," she began, slipping her blond ponytail over one shoulder, "it's pretty easy." Snatching my phone, she entered my four-digit passcode.

About a minute later, she slid it back in front of me. "Done."

"Thank you."

The relief threading through my system felt an awful lot like regret.

She narrowed her eyes at me before resting her fingertips on my now silent phone. "Do you want me to delete the texts he's already sent?"

"Probably should," I answered, my voice breaking on the last word.

I pinched my apple cinnamon cocktail between two fingers and downed the remaining contents. The extra shot of bourbon I'd added burned the entire way down. It was easier to swallow than my disappointment in myself and Will.

Fucking Will.

"That son of a bitch." I groaned.

"I'm sorry," Shay offered, even though she had nothing to apologize for. "I'll be with you when you tell Rose."

"You don't have to."

"I don't want you to do it alone."

If I sank any lower in the booth, I'd be laying down. "How am I gonna tell her?"

There was a band around my chest. To fill my lungs, I had to fight against it.

Across the table, Shay considered me. Her head tilted. Sympathy and kindness warmed her eyes. "Let's not think about it now. I'll text Lawrence that we'll need a ride back to my place."

I snorted. "He loves when we do that."

"He does." A sarcastic smile spread across her lips, and she lifted her empty glass, signaling to Ben behind the bar for another round.

He jerked his chin, before switching tasks to mixing our drinks. It said something about the trashy circumstances when she didn't make a comment about being thirsty for the bartender.

Time was a nebulous thing. I couldn't track it in normal increments. Instead, I judged the passing of time by the near empty drink in my hand. Despite sitting no where near the entrance, frigid wind blasted through the room when the front door swung opened. It was the kind of cold that bit past the heat pouring through the vents. But my blood turned to ice. Shay froze in her booth that turned my blood to ice. Her eyes widened. Her lips parted and her upper lip curled the slightest bit.

Without even looking, I knew.

My sister was here.

Six

Will

Seven nights before Christmas

"The marriage didn't last as long as the wedding planning." It was my canned remark anytime the subject of past relationships came up. First dates and podcast interviews received it well. It brushed over the worst year and a half of my life and made people comfortable. No one ever responded with, *"I'm sorry."* Or, *"That must have been so hard."* Information was received in the manner it was delivered. I didn't seem bothered, so neither were they.

"Hmm." Lizzy considered me. A mahogany ring circled the outside of her brown eyes, an endless circle for me to spiral into.

Before she could say something I didn't have an automatic script for, I asked, "What about you?"

"I had a live-in boyfriend for four years, but when I lost my job, he told me he didn't want to support me while I built my business. I moved in with my parents instead. We didn't last a month in different cities."

"I'm sorry."

"I'm not." She lifted her shoulders and let them fall. "At the time, there'd been so much that needed changing in my life. Broken systems. I should have seen it."

I took a sip from the beer I'd just ordered. The power had restored about forty minutes ago. Neither of us was in a hurry to leave for our rooms. I'd sit there all night if she'd just keep inching her knee a little closer to mine. The anticipation of contact was giving me more of a buzz than the alcohol.

She chewed on her plump lower lip, and my brain fizzled offline. "I can't believe I just told you that."

"Why?"

"I don't think I've told my best friend that."

"Why are you telling me?"

She held my gaze. Her lips were always slightly parted—soft, inviting. The opposite of her icy demeanor. It slowly thawed, and I slipped into the warmth she had just underneath.

I leaned toward her and breathed in the citrus scent of her perfume to hear her airy whisper, "It's probably the stranger in the dark of it all. It feels safe to tell you...things."

Looking over my shoulder, I took in the empty bar. "Not that dark, anymore."

The muscles in her throat flexed. Her words sounded squeezed as she spoke to the straw pinched between her fingertips. "Not much of a stranger anymore."

I rubbed my chest, trying to reach the ache her little vulnerability had put there.

She twirled the straw, tapping it on the bar-top. Her knee bounced near mine. The pink of her cheeks deepened and seeped into the skin of her neck. "I should probably call it a night."

"I should too."

She hesitated to meet my eyes, but when she did, the surrounding air filled with something different. Molecules shifted and adjusted. Energy crackled in the new chemistry. Realizing I'd paused with my beer halfway to my mouth, I lowered it back to the bar.

"I feel..." she trailed off.

I gripped the back of her stool, my hand close enough to feel the heat of her body. The desire to touch her was too much. She had a pull, a magnetism, a gravity. I wanted to sink into the curve of her neck. I could surrender to this attraction. Give in to the tug of her presence, a tightening string wrapping around her finger. It'd been there since the moment I'd sat next to her. The call of her body to mine was a whisper tickling my ear.

"What?" I nearly growled.

"Naked."

She didn't mean undressed. She meant emotionally bare. Exposed. I knew that. But my cock didn't.

I was hard as iron at just the insinuation of this beautiful, intelligent, and guarded woman stripped down. This woman whose last name I didn't know. But I knew the way she blushed when I complimented her on her entrepreneurship. Or how she smiled and rolled her eyes when she told me about her best friend.

I knew like I knew that I needed oxygen to breathe, that I needed to know her.

Clearing my throat, I asked, "Would you feel better if I told you something I don't normally talk about?"

"If you want to." She exhaled a sigh. "Yeah."

I shifted, my sweater suddenly feeling tight. "I... My marriage was the worst time in my life and the divorce was a relief." There was a wrinkle in my beer's label, I couldn't smooth out. "She's a good person, and I think I am, too. But we were toxic together. We kept fucking everything up."

"Why'd you get married?"

It wasn't a question too far, as much as the answer was too complicated. My thumb swiped one last time over the folded ridge of the label.

My chest rose as I sucked in a deep breath of air before blowing it out of my pursed lips.

With a lopsided grin, I turned to face her again. "Should we leave something to unpack for the second date?"

She rolled her lips between her teeth, fighting her smile. Her knee inched a little closer. "We haven't discussed a first date yet."

"How do you feel about hitting fast-forward and calling tonight date number one?"

"Mm-hm."

"I could pick you up from your parents like your prom date," I joked.

She snorted. "God, no."

My smile was too big.

What is this woman doing to me?

"Can I get your phone number?" I would normally find her on Instagram and DM her, but my profile was full of lies at the moment. Comments from strangers celebrating me and Rose announcing our relationship.

It'd been spontaneous, and I was regretting it now. How single had I become that the prospect of meeting someone hadn't even crossed my mind?

Lizzy's eyes flicked to mine. She held her hand palm up, and my fingers grazed hers as I handed her my phone. Electricity shot up my wrist. Her fingertips were cold. I wanted to press them to my neck to warm them. I wanted to brush my lips over them. I wanted to draw a line along her jaw to her mouth with mine.

I shifted, my pants were uncomfortably tight.

She tapped her number into my contacts and handed the phone back.

It sat between us on the bar top, forgotten by the conversation happening between our eyes. Hers questioning and tentative. Mine wanting—offering. After a few silent breaths, she entwined her fingers in mine, our palms pressed together. My other hand gripped white knuckled to the back of her seat.

All my blood rushed to where her knee connected with the inside of my thigh. The anticipation finally brought to volition. Every sensation and thought came from that single point. Sparking, muddled ideas. Half-formed impulses barely restrained.

With each breath, we found space and drifted inch by inch nearer. She tilted her head. Sweet and tart air drifted around her—cranberry from her drinks.

When her lips touched mine, tension broke loose in my chest. A fresh need finally fulfilled.

She sighed, and I felt it in my core.

Seven

Lizzy

SEVEN NIGHTS BEFORE CHRISTMAS

I had never been so bold.

I pressed my palm to Will's. It was just as strong and rough as I'd imagined. I'd started the descent into the space between our mouths. I did that.

Goddamn, boldness was paying off.

Will kissed like my mouth was his last meal, and he needed to savor every taste and texture. Like I was sacred. Invaluable.

It was heady. Drifting on the current of sensations—the ache throbbing between my legs, the heat of his other hand drifting from my back to my hip—my mind blissfully empty. There weren't any self-judgments. They'd evaporated to make room for the bombardment of desire.

Had I ever wanted anything this badly? I didn't know whether to curse this bar for being public or thank it. If we were alone, I would have climbed on his lap by now. Where would his hands go if I straddled him? His mouth?

Then he groaned deep in his throat, and his thumb ran along the tender flesh over my pulse, and I cursed this public place. Fuck this bar. Fuck polite society. I wanted to wrap my naked body around his. If I could will my clothes to disappear, they'd be gone.

If I had magical powers, he wouldn't even own clothes.

I snorted, instantly changing the mood.

He went from inviting ease to stiff backed, and still, all firm muscle—impressively firm...

"That wasn't at you," I whispered.

"It's okay." He pulled back, his green eyes searching mine. "Are you okay?"

"Yes!" I practically screamed three inches from his face. "My God, I didn't mean to yell at you."

One corner of his lips curved up.

I probably should have taken as a sign to relax, but the flutters in my stomach were sharp-edged and there were too many of them. "I thought something funny, and I laughed. But it's not like I meant to laugh. I wasn't laughing at you. I just...laughed."

Crinkles deepened at the corners of his eyes. And thank God he was so pretty. He took the words out of my mouth, when clearly nothing else could have made me stop yapping.

"As long as you're good, I'm good." His words rumbled at the back of his throat. They climbed up my spine.

"You're very good."

Oh my God, woman. Could you pretend you've kissed a man before?

I stood too fast. My face was too hot. I'd been lulled into an unusual state of comfort, and this was the inevitable consequence. People didn't generally like me right away. It took months, sometimes years, for me to let people see me. It was a lesson learned either from my natural introverted nature and anxiety, or because of the loss of the friendship I'd had with my twin sister. A loss that had shaken the very core of me. It'd been eight years, and I was still figuring out who I was if I wasn't someone she loved anymore.

But somehow Will had turned the dial down on the noise in my head. The voice saying, *"That was a weird thing to do with your hands."* Just one faux pas on my part and the voice blasted full volume in my mind.

Fuck. Fuck. Fuck.

"I'm going to go to my room." Then I wondered if that sounded like an invitation, so I added, "Alone."

Eyebrows raised, he blinked.

I couldn't even blame him. He was normal—better than normal. He was like the whisperer of skittish women, or at least, woman. I was the one freaking out.

"Sorry," I whispered. Embarrassingly, my eyes stung.

"You have nothing to apologize for. You don't owe me anything."

"God... please don't be nice."

"I'm not."

I rolled my eyes, and I almost wanted to smile.

"I'm not," he repeated. "I promise."

"Then what are you doing?"

"The bare minimum." He nudged the toe of my boot with his. "It's okay to change your mind."

I pinched my lips together, disappointment a heavy ball in my gut. I hadn't changed my mind. My mind wanted...all of it. Anything Will would give me—a second date, more of that kiss, a tour of his hotel room and naked body.

He tipped back the last of his beer, his Adam's apple bobbed as he swallowed. Setting his empty bottle down, he said, "I have an early day tomorrow. I should head up too."

"Excuse me," he called to the bartender. "Will you charge this to room 1008?"

She nodded and waved.

"You don't have to pay for my drinks." I crossed my arms over my chest.

"Seems like the right thing to do on a first date." He grinned in that unarming way of his. "I'll walk you to the elevators."

He still seemed interested in me, despite my sporadic behavior. I could turn this around.

Be bold, I insisted in my mind. But I'd used up my lifetime supply on one perfect kiss.

Eight

Will

SIX NIGHTS BEFORE CHRISTMAS

I had excused myself to the bathroom fifteen minutes ago. The water I'd splashed dripped from my chin. In the mirror, a face displaying a disturbing combination of horror and disbelief stared back at me. My eyes were too wide, and I couldn't convince my mouth to close.

My blood pressure ratcheted up to the extreme. So much so that just the back door closing startled me.

"This is unbelievable," I kept hissing at my reflection, as if repeating it would make it less true.

I jumped again at a tap on the bathroom door.

"Bill, you good?" Rose asked, her voice muffled by the wooden barrier between us.

I sucked a deep breath in through my nose, scrunching my eyes shut. There was no avoiding this. I had to tell her.

"*Fuck*," I mouthed.

Opening the door, I pulled her in the room with me.

"You need to come out of the bathroom. It's been a weird amount of time," she said, pressing her back to the floral-patterned wallpaper across from the sink.

I scratched at my eyebrow, then ran my hand down my face. Was there a combination of words that could make this less terrible?

I groaned. "You're gonna kill me."

"Why?"

"It's not safe to tell you, because you're gonna kill me."

Rose snorted and rolled her eyes. A behavior so much like Lizzy, I couldn't believe I didn't notice it last night. But the message in the gesture differed between the two of them. Rose's eye roll said, *You're being annoying*, while Lizzy's said, *I haven't decided if you're worth my time.*

Which was my catnip and downfall.

Rose was going to kill me.

"Stop being dramatic and just tell me," she said.

The lip of the counter pressed into my hip. I scraped my palm across my lips, shaking my head.

She considered me out of the corner of her eye. "Okay, you're actually scaring me at this point."

"I'm sorry," I mumbled into my hand. Sighing, I repeated, "I'm really sorry."

I needed to just say it. "I met Lizzy last night."

"Lizzy?"

"Anne."

"My sister?"

"Mm-hmm."

"Where?"

"At the hotel bar."

Rose opened and closed her mouth a few times.

When she finally spoke, there was a threatening edge to her voice. "What do you mean, you *met* her?"

My shoulders hunched, my eyes cast down to the tile floors. "It's as bad as it could be."

In the heavy silence, I forced myself to look at her face. Her cheeks were pink and there was an angry line between her eyebrows.

After a few breaths, she shook her head. "Anne?"

I nodded. "Lizzy."

"I didn't know she had it in her."

"Oh, she had it in her."

Rose lifted the flat of her hand and swung. It smacked against my upper arm. The slap was louder than the sting of contact, but I flinched away.

"Don't be a shithead!" she hiss-whispered, as I whispered back, "Not like that, I didn't mean it like that!"

"How the hell did you mean it?!"

"*I* wasn't the '*it*—'"

"—Ew," she interrupted.

"—I meant that...you know...we were both...*interested*."

"Ew."

"Sorry."

"I'm going to kill you."

"I know."

⚜

After Rose and I shoveled piping hot Shepherd's Pie into our faces, she declared, "We're heading out."

Kelly and Jim shared confused expressions.

"I thought you wanted to stay in," Kelly said. "Relax."

Rose shot me the briefest glare, then forced a smile. "I thought so too. But uh... I really want to show Bill around."

"Okay." Kelly shrugged.

Hustling out the garage door connected to the kitchen felt disrespectful, not just to Kelly and Jim, but to the Shepherd's pie. It was a shame that my taste buds weren't working. Maybe tomorrow I could have leftovers and actually enjoy them. If Rose and Lizzy didn't ship me off in the dark of night like some fugitive.

But necessity justified the quick departure. Rose and I needed to find Lizzy. If I were her, I'd feel used...and gross.

I felt like a shit.

"Text her," Rose directed, sliding into the driver's seat of our rental.

"And say what?" I lifted my hips to pull my phone out of my back pocket.

"I don't know..."

While Rose executed a three-point turn as if we'd stolen the car, I glared at my phone and settled on, *Please let me explain*.

When there wasn't a response, I sent additional texts attempting to explain. It wasn't surprising that they all went unanswered.

"Has she responded to you?" I asked.

Rose turned from her parent's street onto the main road into town. The glow of streetlights a mile away was bright against the dark winter sky. "I haven't texted."

She was sensitive about her sister, so much so that I didn't know the full story of what happened between them. The few times that I'd asked a probing question, Rose had tossed a flippant remark and blown me off. It wasn't the only subject she didn't want to talk about. It was clear that it hurt her more than she was letting on.

I hesitated before asking, "Do you have her number?"

Biting her thumbnail, she scowled at the road. "Of course. You know, in case of an emergency with Mom or Dad."

The click of the blinker banged through the car like a gavel. She took a right to head away from town.

"Where are we going?" I asked.

"She'll be a Shay's."

A few minutes later we parked in the driveway of a simple farmhouse that even in the dark, I could see improvements—newer siding, fresh front porch, updated windows. Details that I noticed subconsciously because of the work Rose and I did.

Lights floated out of the first-floor windows, but I didn't see any movement. We both sat still. Rose's tension mixed with mine.

I shoved my hand through my hair. "You okay?"

She sucked in a breath and held it before blowing it out in a whoosh. "I...I just need to talk to her."

The hinges creaked as Rose pushed the car door open. She was halfway up the walk before I'd even gotten out of my seat. Now that her decision was made, there was no slowing her down. She'd have this talk done and under control. She wouldn't stop pushing and pulling until the situation succumbed to her will.

It was her way.

Her tenacity was truly a beautiful thing, but it could make for certain challenges. Seeing the parts of her personality that fit into place with Lizzy completed a picture I'd only seen half of.

Rose banged four times on the big wooden front door as I bounded up the porch steps. The drone of a grinder went quiet and then heavy steps neared.

Her face went slack and stricken. "Oh, shit."

"What?" I demanded, wondering how anything could get worse.

The door swung open and a tall man in a baseball cap, safety glasses, and a dirty T-shirt stood on the other side.

His eyes widened, and he fell back on his heels as if pushed. "Rosie," he breathed.

Rose's face had gone suspiciously blank, and her voice came out flat. "What are you doing here?"

The smell of sawdust and power tools wafted out with the heat. I peered around him, but instead of seeing signs of Lizzy, there were only a tarp and clip lights hanging around the fireplace.

He lounged against the doorframe. "Workin'. What are you doing here?"

"Looking for Shay and Anne. Are they here?"

"Been a while since you came looking for them." He lifted the neck of his shirt to wipe sweat from his brow. I didn't miss the way Rose's eyes dropped to the skin that showed under the lifted hem. I didn't think he missed it either.

"Sure." A blush warmed her cheeks. "Are they here?"

He shook his head. Extending his hand to me, he said, "Hey man, I'm Lawrence. You must be...Bill?"

I took his hand. "Yeah..."

"Jim told me you were here for the holidays."

"Lawrence works for my dad," she explained. "So, they're not here."

"No."

"'Kay." She turned on her heels and started back toward the car.

He and I shared an awkward wave goodbye. I jogged with my hands in the pockets of my leather coat to the car. Rose had both hands on the steering wheel, her seat belt already buckled, by the time I closed my door.

"So that's the ex-boyfriend?" I asked.

"Yup." She nodded at the now vacant front porch.

We were in a terrible fake relationship.

Nine

Lizzy

SIX NIGHTS BEFORE CHRISTMAS

"Rosie!" I heard Ben greeting my sister as if my head were underwater. Blood rushed in my ears. My arms and legs grew cold and sluggish as my lungs filled with hot air and my cheeks burned.

There was a back door. It was in sight. I could dash for it.

I wasn't ready to tell Rose. Not here. Not among all these people to see us, and whisper about us around town. She'd hate that.

I'd hate that.

"Hey Benji," she chirped back, her voice close to the booth. I expected her to go to the bar or to an empty table, but she slid into the seat next to me. "Can you bring a fresh round for Anne and Shay, and whatever light beer you have on tap for us?"

I'd already stopped breathing the second Rose's hip bumped mine, demanding more space without saying a word. Making room for her was second nature—a behavior I'd done since in utero. But all my bodily functions failed, my heart stopped, and my brain sputtered to a halt when a hand gripped the corner of our backrest by Rose's shoulder.

It only made sense that Will, of the beautiful hands and philandering bullshit, would be with her, but I was not ready.

"Breathe, Anne," she commanded. A thud sounded under the table, and Shay winced. "Fix your face, Shay. We aren't killing him tonight."

I didn't know what to make of Rose's calm, commanding demeanor. Her sitting next to me, talking to me...it was something I'd wanted for so long that I'd stopped acknowledging the ache of her distance. Now that she was here, I was even more confused. It didn't make sense that she'd know about me and Will.

Cheating boyfriends rarely admitted to their girlfriends, right?

How could she know when I still hadn't told her?

"Night's still young," Shay hissed, glaring at Will. I couldn't bring myself to look at him. Instead, I focused on the gleaming grain of the tabletop.

"Everyone, calm down—" Rose started.

As I said, "I have to tell you—"

"—No, you don't," she interrupted. "Bill already did. It's okay."

Shay crossed her arms on the table. "What exactly did he tell you?"

"He told me about last night."

Tears stung my eyes. I blinked down at my lap, willing them to go away.

Mimicking her body language, Rose leaned on the tabletop too. "I really need you to bring your over protectiveness down a notch, okay?"

Balancing all four drinks in his hands, Ben stopped next to where Will stood. He pretended not to notice the weird tension in our group. I was sure he did, though. That was why everyone came to Benji's, because he and his waitstaff acted as if they were oblivious to local drama.

He distributed the drinks before he and Rose hugged. "Good to see ya."

"You too. The bar looks great," she offered.

"Thank you. It's a work in progress, but it keeps getting a little better every year." Turning his attention, he held out his hand. "You're Bill."

"Sometimes he goes by *Will*." Shay said his name like a dirty word, dripping venom, drawing it out into two syllables.

Ben's eyebrow twitched before he pretended as if she hadn't spoken. "I've watched some of your videos. You two are cute together."

The knife in my gut twisted. I would have known who Will was if I paid attention to my sister's Internet presence. But a para-social relationship was salt in the wound. I'd learned years ago that it was better for my mental state to not seek her out. Not to google her or scroll through her social media profiles. It hurt too much.

That really backfired.

I couldn't keep track of time or follow the conversation over the buzzing in my ears, but it didn't seem like Ben stuck around for long.

When he walked away, Rose put a hand on my wrist. I forced myself to meet her eyes.

"Bill and I aren't actually dating," she whispered.

Wrinkles crossed Shay's forehead. But Rose's shoulders remained confidently set. Against my better judgement, my eyes landed on Will's face and found his mossy green gaze fixed on me with concern and apology fitted into their softened corners. My heart ached, forcing me to look away.

Rose continued in a lowered voice. She explained about an agent shopping their YouTube channel to streaming services, and her and Will's attempt to appear more desirable by giving their audience the relationship they'd always wanted to see.

"It *officially* started this morning," she explained. Will winced at her emphasis on the word 'officially'.

"It's not real." She turned in her seat, giving me all her attention. "Everything is okay."

"How long are you two going to do this?" Shay asked.

"I don't know." Rose looked up at Will, but I still hadn't processed the information well enough to venture a second look in his direction. "We were thinking either a week or two before or after Valentine's."

Shay leaned in closer. "That doesn't make any sense. If a streaming service picks up your show because you're pretending to be in this cute little relationship—"

"Not because of the relationship. Because of the hype. A breakup is also hypey."

"Unless the breakup makes your audience turn on you."

"They won't do that."

Shay raised a skeptical brow.

"You can't tell anyone, Shay."

"Anyone? Or just Lawrence?"

Rose's lips pressed into a tight line. "*Anyone.*"

"Lizzy." Will's voice broke through the noise of the bar and the ringing in my ears.

Like a moth to a flame, my eyes found his. His lips set in a stern line. His focus pinned me to the booth. I could practically feel the weight of his body on mine. The clean scent of his soap mixing with the sharp smell of our sweat. On my upper thigh, my skin tingled at the bruises his fingers had left.

"I'm sorry," he said.

"If you did nothing wrong, why are you apologizing?" Shay challenged.

For just a moment, he looked at her, and I missed the pressure of his eyes. I was such a fool for wanting his attention, but I did. This was messier than meeting a man in a bar. This was messier than a one-night stand. This would only get messier by me wanting him.

"I made her feel fucking terrible." His eyes found me once more, tugging me toward him all over again. "I'm sorry."

The tight string bound around my chest loosened. A little consolation prize that at least I hadn't read him wrong.

I jerked my head toward Shay. "Can he sit with you?"

She heaved a tremendous sigh, then scooted further into her booth.

"Thanks," he mumbled.

He assessed my smeared mascara and pink nose. A muscle flexed in his jaw, and I could read his regret in the set of his brows.

Jerking his chin toward the drink in front of me, he said, "That's not a vodka cranberry."

"Last night might have ruined them for me." I smirked down at the table. "Maybe I'll only drink them during power outages."

The corners of his mouth twitched up.

It took a few moments for me to notice Shay and Rose glancing between us, followed by Shay pursing her lips.

Messy, a little voice in my head urged. Even as I relaxed my guard a further.

"So, how did you find us, anyway?" Shay asked.

If I hadn't been sitting so close to Rose, I might have missed the way she tensed. Her voice remained deceptively calm. "We went to your house first."

Shay's lip curled, and I imagined she was fed up with all of us. "You saw Lawrence?"

"Yes, I saw him." Rose looked down at her white, sparkly painted nails. "Don't worry, he's still in one piece."

Just under her breath, Shay mumbled, "I doubt it."

Will sent me a questioning look that flipped my stomach upside down. He took my shrug for an answer.

In unison, the four of us lifted our beverages and swallowed long drinks.

Ten

Will

FIVE NIGHTS BEFORE CHRISTMAS

Being a gentleman was the damned worst. My entire body was sore from sleeping on the floor—but it'd be too weird to share a bed with Rose. So, I'd made a pathetic nest on the carpet with as many extra blankets and pillows as we could sneak into the spare bedroom without her parents noticing.

I stretched my arm across my chest and my shoulder cracked while Rose drooled on a pillow that looked like a cloud. Stepping into the hallway, I resisted shaking her awake out of vengefulness.

I followed the smell of coffee to the kitchen. Only to find Lizzy.

Her hair was in a bun on top of her head, and she wore a burgundy robe tied around her waist. Fluffy slippers covered her feet. Her ankles were bare. So bare...

I didn't think I'd ever been more aware of another person's ankles. I felt like an olden times pervert, lusting over the smooth skin peaking between her slippers and pajama pants.

"Good morning." She swiped a hand over the wild strands of her hair curling around her shoulders.

I cleared my throat, but my voice still sounded scraped with gravel with my reply. "Good morning."

With a mug covered in cat faces, she gestured over her shoulder. "There's coffee," she said, at the same time I said, "I smelled coffee."

My smile was a mirror of hers—small, embarrassed, careful.

The night before, I'd finished my beer while trying not to notice the adorable pink that filled Lizzy's cheeks every time I looked at her. Shay and Rose did most of the talking—something about a decorating competition. The conversation didn't capture my attention long enough to retain any details.

Her gaze cast down to her slipper covered toes, and my heart ached. This was not how I wanted to know her. If this were a different morning, I'd have woken up next to her. Or I'd find her in the kitchen and pull her against my chest, breathe in the floral scent of her hair. The same smell I'd been craving since I had her underneath me in a hotel bed.

The memory washed over me like electric sparks on my skin. I closed my eyes to it, but there was no blocking out the remembered taste of her on my tongue or the way her thighs twitched over my shoulders.

"Are you okay?" The floor creaked as she took a step closer.

Stuffing my hand in the pocket of my basketball shorts, I adjusted the very sudden and very unwelcome semi.

When I opened my eyes, she was still a few feet away. Her brown gaze concerned, and her soft, pink lips parted. She must have interpreted the path my thoughts had wandered down because her eyes flicked down to my shorts.

Her mouth pulled into a silent, *"Oh."*

Under my fingernails, the stubble on my neck rustled with my nervous scratching. "Sorry."

She covered her mouth with her free hand, clearly hiding a smile.

"Is this funny?"

She lifted one shoulder. "Boners are funny," she whispered.

I snorted, and she pressed her finger to her lips to shush me. We contained our laughter from growing too loud. The shame and betrayal I'd seen in her eyes the night before was gone. Replaced by a secret that only we shared. A silliness that did nothing to quell my growing...*problem*.

"You're not helping the situation," I groaned, forcing myself to not close the distance between us.

"I'm not even doing anything."

"You don't have to."

"Should I go back to my room?"

Self-preservation would say, *yes*. What good could come from this? Was there a reality where Lizzy and I could have more than a hidden fling some day?

But the golden morning sunlight cast her in shades I didn't want to turn away from, so I shook my head.

Her teeth pressed into her lower lip. "Why don't you take a seat at the counter while you...take care of that."

"Take care of it?"

"I don't know...*tend* to it?"

"At the kitchen counter?"

She struggled to control the smile dominating her face and lost. "You know what I mean."

Placing the island between us, I sat on the stool and tapped my fingers on the quartz countertop. "Don't mind me, I'm *tending*."

She giggled, her cheeks turning bright pink. "Stop it. How do you like your coffee? I'll grab it for you."

"Lots of cream, little sugar."

She opened the refrigerator door. I watched her move around the kitchen. She stretched up onto her toes to grab a mug, revealing more of her slutty ankles. It didn't take long before she set a full, steaming cup in front of me.

"Thank you."

"You're welcome."

I held her gaze as I lifted the liquid to my mouth, taking a sip as she took a drink of hers. The delicate muscles of her neck flexed.

What I wouldn't give to scrape my teeth up the tender skin of her throat—

"Good morning," Jim—her *dad*—greeted us.

Somehow, I didn't sputter my coffee in my surprise, instead I swallowed way too much, and it burned the entire way down. I blinked back the tears filling my eyes.

On the plus side, my erection had practically deflated.

"Morning," Lizzy chirped, her shoulders rigid. "How'd you sleep?"

"Fine. Thanks for brewing coffee, sweetheart."

"Sure thing!"

"Mornin', Will."

I nodded my head once. "Jim," I groaned, my throat still burning.

"I see you met Lizzy."

"At the bar," she explained, then a little too quickly she added, "*last* night."

"Is that where you two ran off to?" He directed the question to me.

"Yup." I coughed once into my fist. "Nice place."

"It is. That Ben is a smart young man. You all doin' the Christmas Tree Decorating Contest today?"

Lizzy shifted her weight to one hip and raised an eyebrow at her dad. "You think Mom and Rose would sit this out?"

"Them? No. But you do some years."

"I'll tag along."

"Wait..." I scowled into the middle distance, the inkling of a memory tickling the back of my mind. "Would there be a vision board for this? Something to do with... What is that ballet?"

They exchanged a vexed glance before answering in unison, "Swan Lake."

Jim shook his head. "There are so many feathers in my basement."

"And other design elements," Rose said through a yawn. She padded barefoot to kiss her dad on the cheek. "Morning, Anne."

Lizzy blinked, her mug paused on the way to her lips. "Good morning."

"What about your young man? No kiss to start his day?" Jim asked. He might have been joking but judging by Rose's deer-in-the-headlights expression, she had experienced the same jolt of terror that I had.

"It-it's okay," I stammered. "We already did, in the bedroom."

She tilted her head saying without saying, *What the fuck?*

"Not like *that*," I rambled on.

Jim's eyebrows shot up.

"You know, not like *that*."

"Yes, son, I believe I know."

"Yeah, *you* know."

"Oh my God," Rose groaned, her palm pressed to her forehead.

"Why did you emphasize 'you' like that?" Lizzy asked.

And lord help me, there was the sweetest affection set in her warm eyes. It was the lifeline I needed to close my mouth—to stop digging deeper into the humiliating hole I was about six-feet deep in.

"If I kiss you, will you stop talking?" Rose had already rounded the kitchen island. Placing her hands on both sides of my face, she turned my head toward her and away from Lizzy.

Then her tightly closed mouth was on mine.

And it was...not good.

Eleven

Lizzy

FIVE NIGHTS BEFORE CHRISTMAS

I thought Rose and Will kissing would be painful because of jealousy, and it was. My sister's lips pressed to his brought out a possessiveness I hadn't felt. But it was more painful for completely different reasons. They didn't just look like they'd never kissed one another; they looked like they'd never kissed *anyone*.

Their movements were stiff and jerky. First, they jammed their faces together. Then they pulled away too far apart, before bopping back together. It was no less embarrassing than Will's rambling and, at least, that had been cute.

This was not cute.

If I hadn't already kissed him and knew exactly how hot it was. This display would convince me to never let his mouth touch mine.

It wasn't just the kiss that was unnatural. I hadn't made such an instantaneous and stark connection with anyone. Ever. Pretending to have just met was like denying an instinct.

Rose lowered to the stool next to him. Our little group hovering in the kitchen avoided eye contact, as if we'd shared in a trauma.

I scraped at the dregs of my mind, searching for anything to say—a change of subject, a random thought, *anything*.

"I'm gonna see if your mom is up." Dad hurried out of the room, his mug of coffee gripped in one hand.

I ignored how unusual it was to speak directly to Rose after so many years of silence. "If you want to convince anyone this is legit, don't do that again."

Shaking her head at the countertop, Rose agreed, "I don't think either of us wants to repeat that."

Will's eyebrows rose toward his hairline. "No, thank you."

The basement of the Methodist Church was half classrooms and one large gathering room. It was the size of a small gymnasium with gleaming tile that reflected the fluorescent lights overhead. Along the cinderblock walls was a row of plain pine trees, donated by a local orchard. The space smelled the same as it did every single year. A strange savory scent, as if so many luncheons, birthday parties, weddings and funeral receptions had baked the aroma of pulled pork into the walls. Add a dash of cinnamon air fresheners and pine and the combination wasn't unappealing. But it was strange.

Mom and Rose had stationed me next to their tree of choice. It was a good foundation for their vision, according to Mom. Then they'd dashed up the stairs to the car, dragging Will along. He slowly descended into my line of sight, a box of feathers and twigs almost completely covering his face.

"Follow the sound of my voice," I called into the vacant room.

I could hear his smile, even hidden. "*Marco.*"

"*Polo.*"

His boots clicked on the tile, echoing off the walls. Placing the box on the floor, he put his hands on his hips and considered the tree, then the rest of the room. The breadth of his ribcage stretching his navy henley did something to the air in my lungs—too hot, too thick.

Out of the corner of his eye, he shot me a knowing glance. Heat rose into my cheeks. I looked away chewing on my lower lip.

He scraped thick, square fingers across his mouth. After a breath, he asked, "Is your mom as competitive as Rose?"

The change of subject—start of subject?—was welcome. "Oh yeah. They get way too intense about this."

He cringed. "Good. Good."

"It doesn't help that every year it's neck and neck between them and Shay's family."

"Your friend from last night?"

I nodded.

"She's got a mean glare."

"It's not fun to be on the receiving end. You handled it well."

He rubbed a hand on the back of his neck, his biceps flexed under his long sleeve. The soft cotton hugged the contours of his muscles, and I lost track of all my cohesive thoughts.

"It was," he started, a quiet, tentative hesitation braided into his words, "worth it...to make you feel better."

I grinned down at my toes. He was too cute and sweet. I wanted to dive headfirst into all the feelings he brought to the surface. The sensitive ones that I usually kept hidden. The ones that I was usually afraid of because of how they left me vulnerable.

"Do you feel better?" he asked.

"I do...but I felt pretty shitty last night."

"I bet."

I forced my face to remain neutral, concealing the depth of my remembered pain. "No, yeah, don't worry about it."

"Sure, but this whole thing feels unfair. You didn't sign up for all of this, it was just kinda hoisted on you."

He wasn't wrong. But I didn't know how to receive the sentiment. Fighting back tears at Benji's last night to flirting over coffee was a harsh transition, yet I could bring myself to regret it as far as I could resist his charm.

Then there was the aspect of being included in Rose's life—not that it was something she'd chosen. It didn't really matter, though. I would take the scraps if it meant that maybe we could—

I didn't know what, but it seemed like a step toward something better.

"Do you have any siblings?" I asked out of nowhere, and he blinked in surprise before shaking his head.

I shrugged. "It won't be the first time I've lied for her. I'm willing to."

I left out that I was almost happy to do it.

"Has she ever lied for you?"

I snorted. "Oh, yeah."

His thick eyebrows shot up, wrinkles creased his forehead. "A lot?"

"Well...probably not as much as I have for her. But one time when we were eighteen, I spent a weekend in Montreal without our parents knowing. She thought it was a terrible idea, but she covered for me, anyway."

"It was a terrible idea."

"Absolutely, but isn't what you're doing a bad idea too?"

"Touché. Why Montreal?"

"A boy."

"Were you safe?"

"Yes. I was smart enough to have safety measures in place, but I didn't end up needing them."

"Was it fun?"

"No. It was so awkward."

He considered me for a moment. "You two used to be close?"

My throat tightened. I forced out, "Yes."

"What happened?"

Surprisingly, I wanted to answer him. The truth as I saw it sat right at the tip of my tongue before I stopped myself. It would violate Rose's trust. "You should talk to her."

He opened his mouth, but the thud of footsteps coming down the stairs cut him off.

Shay and Lawrence's arms hung low at their sides with reusable grocery bags full of decorations.

I looked back at Will. We were standing close enough that I could see the shape of his eyelashes and the uneven points of his cupid's peak. I took a big step back, but not soon enough to miss the pinch of Lawrence's eyebrows or the warning glare Shay fixed on Will.

Shit.

They took the tree next to ours, and gave us awkward, half-hearted, hellos. It was a relief when their mom came down with her bright energy and warm hugs. Soon after, the church basement was loud with the sounds of people talking and kids squealing. Mom and Rose discussed in quick, clipped whispers about the possible placements of this object or that. A plan growing on how best to use the tree's natural empty spots and testing the strength of the limbs.

Will and I shared a rueful glance.

"It might be best if we just stay out of the way," I suggested.

"I'll keep us in hot chocolate," he offered.

They announced the beginning of the competition, and the place erupted in a flurry of ornaments and garland. The whole time, it was as if there was a Lawrence sized blind spot in Rose's vision. If he stood to her right, she looked to her left.

When she bumped into Will with feathers clasped in both hands, he took a big step back. "I'm gonna go get those hot chocolates."

I would have joined him, but I had an ornament dangling on each finger just waiting for my mom to pluck one off. He weaved through the crowd a few minutes later. Balancing four paper cups in his hands, he paused at a gasp from Ms. Patricia. Her blue eyes lined in their customary black eyeliner.

"Your Rose's Bill!" she exclaimed.

His eyes shot to mine for the barest moment. His smile was tight and forced. "Uh, yeah. I am. Nice to meet you."

Tilting my head down, I drew my toe along a line separating two tiles. My stomach was suddenly queasy.

"We're big fans—me and my daughter, Jamie. We've been rootin' for you two for so long."

"Thank you."

"We were just over the *moon* when we found out you two were *finally* dating."

Every one of her sentences deepened his cheeks into a darker shade of pink. My thoughts jumbled. The connection between the Will who could be mine and this Bill who belonged to Rose in the eyes of everyone else tangled together like Christmas lights.

"Thank you," he said again.

"We follow you on everything, so we knew you were in town because of that picture on your stories yesterday."

"Right, yeah." He swallowed. "What do you do?"

She pressed a hand to her chest, her red fingernails bright against her green sweater. "I manage the humane society."

"Oh, cool."

"You know, it'd mean the world to us if you could come by before you leave. Take a couple of pictures of you and the animals. Something for us to post and drive up donations and adoptions. Even after Hazel's big fundraiser in October, we're always looking for help."

"Right, yeah, sure. I'm sure we can find time."

"Aren't you wonderful! When do you think you can?"

"Let me talk to Rose. In fact," he lifted the cups in his hands, "one of these is hers. I should probably get it to her."

"Okay, don't forget about me, though."

"I won't."

"Promise?"

"I promise."

She reached up and patted him on the shoulder. "You're just as sweet as you seem on your show."

"'Preciate it."

Jerking her head toward my mom and sister and their focus on their task, she added, "Watch out for those two. They're mostly harmless, but they take this very seriously."

One corner of his mouth lifted, making him look more like the man I'd gotten to know. "I understand."

He set two of the cups on the little table pushed into the corner. The hot chocolate he extended toward me smelled sweet. I glanced down at my hands, that had sprouted even more ornaments.

His chuckle set my heart to a different rhythm.

"It's not actually hot. I could hold it for you." There was a golden ring around his pupil. It must have been the lighting that made it seem brighter, and nothing to do with the yearning tug of his gaze on mine.

I glanced from side to side. Mom and Rose had dashed up the stairs to grab something from Mom's van. Tucked into the corner behind the tree, we were mostly hidden. Not that there was anything wrong with him holding a cup for me. If anyone saw us, they probably wouldn't think anything of it.

But I knew.

I wasn't desperate for the taste of chocolate on my tongue. I wasn't thirsty. I didn't need what was in that cup.

It was Will.

His mossy green eyes locked onto my lips pinched between my teeth.

"I could use a drink," I said, and if my voice was a bit breathy, I didn't blame me.

A muscle flexed in his jaw. He took a step closer. Just close enough that I could barely catch the clean scent of his skin. His pulse thrummed against his throat.

Holding the cup a few inches from my face, he directed, "Tilt your head back."

I blinked out of my daze, suddenly aware of my caramel-colored cashmere sweater and the potential of a stain. "You won't spill, right?"

A smile split his face, and I stopped caring if I ended up wearing the whole ten-ounce cup.

Just pour it on me.

"No, I won't spill. Actually, here." He stepped even closer. A shiver ran down my spine as his strong fingers plunged into the hair at the nape of my neck. He placed the cup on my lower lip and eased my head back.

My senses were full of his firm grip, and creamy chocolate, and the focus of his eyes on my mouth.

It was over as quickly as it started.

I swallowed the liquid. Overwhelmed and bereft.

He'd taken steps away. His chest rose and fell with deep breaths. My breathing a match for his. I didn't have to press my hand to his chest to know that our hearts beat at the same pace. We were trapped in the same maze, twists and turns and dead ends separated us. But we were pulled toward the same center.

His eyes raked over me. The way his eyes drew over the curves of my body was as if, instead of a loose-fitting sweater and jeans, I was wearing nothing at all.

When he met my gaze again, the force of his need pushed the air from my lungs. Then he lifted the cup he'd just held to my lips. Without breaking eye contact, he put it to his mouth, tilted his head back, and drank.

❧❧❧❧❧ ❧❧❧❧❧

A little over an hour later, glitter littered the floor, and they'd announced the winner of the contest. But I struggled to break from the loop of Will and that damn cup of hot chocolate.

Nothing that erotic had happened in the basement of the Methodist Church before.

Once again, I found myself to be the only person standing next to "our" tree. But in truth, it was Mom's and Rose's accomplishment.

It was stunning.

The longer I looked at it, the more I appreciated the depth and thought they'd put into it. Heavily interspersed feathers cascaded from top to bottom making the tree looked like it might take flight. The white elements were heavier in the lower branches and grew blacker as they ascended. There was even a dancer twirling on a mirror lake tucked near the trunk. Rose's handmade topper, depicting a delicate ballerina draped in white tulle and feathers, of course, with the same ballerina done in black emerging ominously from behind her. The display was opulent and ridiculous.

It was possibly my favorite tree they'd ever done.

I recognized Rose's footfalls descending the stairs. My shoulders tensed, and I breathed through my pursed lips to force my tight chest to loosen. Every time she had ignored me in the past dug little divots out of my heart. But something had shifted in the past twenty-four hours.

It hurt to hope.

"Hey," she mumbled, but it bounced off the cinderblock walls and tile floor.

"Hi," I answered.

"What are you doing?"

Shrugging one shoulder, I looked back to her tree. "Appreciating..."

Saying the word *art* felt pretentious, even if that was exactly what she and Mom had created.

Rose crossed her arms over her chest, standing a few feet to my left. She took in the bulbs and feathers with a more critical eye than mine. "We were a bit heavy-handed—"

"It's perfect," I cut her off. "You were robbed."

We both looked at the winning Christmas tree, with its Santa's Train theme. Shay, Lawrence, and their mom had done an excellent job. It was wholesome and sweet.

"I do love to win, but I'd rather make this," Rose gestured to her creation with the flick of a wrist, "than that."

"They did a good job."

"It's cute," she acknowledged.

I fixed my gaze pointedly on the black swan prima donna sitting atop the tree. She stared back with disdain and judgment. "And it's not even a little frightening to small children."

She chuckled. "So, like, what even is the point, then?"

I laughed. "Seriously. Now this," I pointed up to the tree, "some kid is going to remember."

"This is core memory material."

We snorted in unison. A little bridge built across the great divide between us, at once intimidating and optimistic.

Have you missed me like I've missed you? I wanted to ask, but I swallowed the words down.

I would take it one snort at a time.

Twelve

Will

FIVE NIGHTS BEFORE CHRISTMAS

"Can I ask you a question?" I laid on my back, grateful that it was my night on the mattress. Rose had offered to switch every other night—it was her turn on the floor nest.

The moon reflected off the snow outside the window, casting the shadow of a tree's limbs on the ceiling. It's bent twigs and branches, creating a pattern of white diamonds.

After the contest, we'd had dinner with Lizzy and their parents. I spent the entire time wondering if I was engaging a normal "I'm Dating Your Sister" amount with Lizzy, and not a "Jesus Christ I'm Tormented by the Way You Tilt Your Head When You Think" amount.

Then we'd gone downstairs to the family room to watch Prancer because, "It was the girls' favorite!" according to their mom. Rose tested putting her feet on my lap—not good. I stared at a curl resting on the nape of Lizzy's neck until Rose kicked my thigh. Her scowl clearly conveying, *Stop being creepy.*

Also, not good.

But the memory of those strands curling around my fingers was vivid. Just a few hours before, I'd had my hands on Lizzy. Her neck exposed. Her lips pursed. The soft fabric of her sweater draped across the full peaks of her breasts.

Resisting my attraction was impossible. My only hope was avoiding Lizzy.

But then Rose invited her to join us at their cousin's stables tomorrow before the holiday party for their mom and dad's business. Lizzy lit up with surprise and...something I could only describe as joy. A bright, beautiful burst of pink on her cheeks and a sparkle in her mahogany eyes. It'd been there every time Rose included Lizzy in a conversation or acknowledged her.

I liked to give Rose her space. She kept her cards close to her chest, even with me. Privacy was important to her, but my curiosity was too loud.

It was possible that I was too protective of Lizzy too.

"Sure," Rose answered. Her apprehensive voice came from the floor around my shoulder.

"What happened between you and Lizzy?"

"Did she tell you something?"

"Just that I should talk to you."

Rose grunted, then fell silent. The ticking of the clock hanging on the wall was the only sound. It rang out the passing of time like a hammer driving a nail.

Finally, Rose sighed. "We were supposed to go to State together. Then I dropped it on everyone that I was going to St. Lawrence instead."

I scowled at the ceiling. "That doesn't seem too bad."

"It really wasn't. But she and Lawry were really pissed—he was about to start his sophomore year, and the long-distance relationship was shitty. He was expecting me to join him at State, too."

"You were dating him at the time?"

"Yeah, sorry. I'm not telling this story well." Her voice had a suspiciously shaky quality. "Anyway, it was the end of that relationship. But...um...she felt betrayed, too. And I thought, you know, she didn't really have the right to—I didn't really *do* anything."

I made a grunting sound, not ready to agree or disagree.

"Anyway, hindsight is twenty, twenty, right?"

"What do you see in hindsight?"

"I did betray her." She said it bluntly, with a hollow lack of emotion. "She made her plans, expecting me to be there. I don't think she was ready to be without me, and I forced it on her. Mom said she struggled, her grades suffered. We weren't talking by the time Christmas break rolled around, but I could see she was depressed. There was this shell around her. She looked so tired. And she hardly laughed."

Something gripped my chest, thinking of Lizzy young and alone.

"We'd done the silent treatment before," Rose continued. "It'd never gone on that long, though. When I tried talking to her, she glared at me and asked if I was ready to apologize yet."

"I'm guessing you weren't."

She scoffed. "No, I was not."

"But why are you two still like this? That was so long ago."

Instead of answering, Rose whispered, "Can I tell you something truly fucking terrible?"

"You can tell me."

She breathed deeply and held it, as if she couldn't quite catch her breath. "I think I've wasted a lot of time wanting to be right. Not *right*, I guess. I wanted to not be *wrong*. I wanted it to be her fault that we weren't friends anymore. That we were barely tied together.

"She just wanted an apology. And I wouldn't do it. So, I...I was so self-righteous, and all she wanted was for me to say, sorry. I shut her out for *years*. She tried, and I was such a *bitch*—"

"Don't call yourself that," I interrupted. Rose had been wrong to let it go this long, but she wasn't an evil person. "What do you mean, 'she tried'?"

"She invited me to hangout. I'd tell her I was busy, whether I was or not. She can tell when I'm lying, just like I can tell when she is. Eventually, she stopped trying. I never even started."

Rose sniffled.

"You could still. If you wanted to," I suggested. Grief was thick in the room. It weighed down the atmosphere, pressing into my sternum. My heart ached for these two sisters experiencing so much loss when they were under the same roof.

"I do. I want to make it right. But I can see how much I have hurt her. How that pain carved her out. Years on years of this. I want to fix us, but I've done so much damage."

"Have you ever said sorry?"

"Too little too late, don't you think?"

"Maybe not."

She let out a watery laugh. "I talked so much shit. To anyone who would listen, I made it out like she was some codependent weirdo who was obsessed with me. Instead of a scared eighteen-year-old who hadn't realized that her twin sister was going to abandon her for a new life."

"That sucks."

"It does."

I didn't press her further. After a while, Rose's tightly controlled breathing turned to snoring.

Eventually, I fell asleep wondering if Lizzy was okay.

Thirteen

Will

SEVEN NIGHTS BEFORE CHRISTMAS

"Do you think it's safe to use the elevator?" Lizzy asked with her arms crossed over her chest. She chewed on her lower lip with her eyebrows drawn together.

I wobbled my head from side to side. "There's a risk the power could go out, again. What floor are you on?"

"Seventh."

"I don't want to climb seven flights of stairs—"

"Me either."

"—but I'd do it with you." I gave her a little smirk. "You have to promise not to laugh at me when I'm breathing really heavy."

She did that adorable snort she'd done a couple of times. "I'd be too busy trying not to die. No, let's risk the elevator."

Her tentative little smile pulled at the dusty levers of my heart. Her kiss had been all warmth and quiet sighs. With every protective layer that thawed, I caught a glimpse of the passionate woman underneath.

It provoked *everything* in me. I wanted to pull her tight against my chest and be some place she felt safe. I wanted to search for all the ways to unravel her tightly wound persona. I wanted to *know* her.

I wouldn't tell her any of that.

It was a lot—too much for just a few hours of conversation and a single kiss.

But secretly, I harbored an unhealthy amount of hope for what we could be.

I should tell her about *Will it Bloom? Renovations* and how Rose and I were shopping the show for streaming services. It would be better than Lizzy somehow googling me and thinking that everything tonight was a lie. Especially since I had never had such an honest encounter. I'd never bared myself so completely.

Maybe I could hold this one thing back and trust that it wouldn't blow up in my face.

My boots thudded on the tile floor, and hers clicked as we made our way to the elevators right around the corner. I slipped my hand from my pocket and pushed the button to call it to the main floor. A bell chimed and the stainless-steel doors slid open. I followed her into the cabin, wishing that I had more than the next few seconds with her.

I wouldn't wish for the power to fail, but being trapped here with Lizzy would be a silver lining.

She rounded to the buttons, and I leaned my back against the opposite wall. I took in the sight of her. She was the manifestation of all my preferences—full curves and thick thighs, chestnut colored hair, and round brown eyes. And, of course, the prickly outer shell that I wanted to get beneath.

She looked at me through her lashes. "Tenth floor, right?"

"Mmm-hm." I nodded.

She breathed in, her breasts rose and press against the neckline of her sweater. A blush pinked her cheeks. There was no end to how she charmed me.

"You're beautiful, Lizzy," I whispered, my words almost lost in the sliding of the doors.

"Thank you."

We started our ascent.

I resisted the urge to tell her I didn't want to say goodnight, but just barely.

She gripped the railing at her hips in both hands, facing me. "Tonight doesn't feel totally real."

"No, it doesn't," I agreed.

The floors ticked by. Each one announced that our meeting was ending, level three, four, five.

"Come here." I held my hand out to her. She took it, closing the space between us in two long strides.

I pulled her against me. My hand fit at her waist. The material of her sweater was soft beneath my palm. Her mouth found mine with the same urgency that I felt. She tilted her head, giving me room to deepen our connection, and I took it. I was too far gone for anything but the taste of her, the feel of her. The way her breasts pressed against my chest. She met my need with her own.

She moaned deep in her throat. My cock twitched against her stomach, and she whimpered. I growled a response. Turning, I pinned her between me and the wall. I might have wondered if that was too far, but she hooked her leg around my thigh and my thoughts vanished.

I was losing myself in the heat of her seeping into my hip, when the ring of a bell declared that we were at her floor. The elevator doors slid open, and the cocoon wrapped around us tore open. Laughing and talking barraged into the cabin as a group of women waited on the other side of the doors.

Pulling away from Lizzy went against every instinct in my body.

The sounds of the strangers died out, replaced by a cough that did nothing to disguise laughter.

Lizzy smoothed a hand over her hair, but her ponytail hung loose. Her lips were swollen and the heat in her eyes stoked the fire already burning inside of me.

"I will call you." I promised, forcing myself to take a step back.

She swallowed. "Good night."

Her hips swayed as she strode past the women, sharing gossipy glances. My heart raced, and I struggled against the urge to chase after her. Eventually, the doors slid shut before the elevator carried me up the last few floors.

Alone.

Wondering how something could be this intense and consuming. How could I be head over heals so quickly?

Fourteen

Lizzy

SEVEN NIGHTS BEFORE CHRISTMAS

The door swung open.

I'd more or less ran from the elevator to knock on room 1008, out running my thoughts and second guessing. Sending out a prayer that I'd remembered his room number correctly. As soon as my knuckles hit the...whatever hotel doors were made of, there was no turning back. My stomach twisted in knots, then sank to my knees as Will blinked back his surprise. When he smiled, I floated.

"Lizzy," he sighed. Running a hand through his mussed-up hair, he stepped back to let me in.

He'd discarded his sweater, leaving him in his jeans and a white t-shirt. It clung to his pecs and shoulders, and I had to drag my gaze back to his. The man could fill out a scrap of cotton.

"Is it okay I'm here?" I asked, rubbing a thumb on the strap of my toiletry bag. "I didn't want to say goodnight."

"Me either."

His room was just like mine. A hallway from the door to an open space with a king-sized bed, a television mounted next to a large mirror. A sunny lake scene hung above his headrest—mine was an abstract print of flowers, but otherwise everything was the same. His brown leather coat draped over the chair in the corner next to his suitcase unzipped on the floor.

I set my little bag on the table under the mirror. It suddenly seemed presumptuous to bring it. Turning, I crossed my arms over my chest. "I was scared that I remembered your room number wrong."

Throwing his head back, he laughed at the ceiling. The sound was so full, and it pulled the corners of my lips. I leaned back against the table, gripping the edge of it in both hands, resisting the urge to hug him.

Why is he so magnetic?

"You got it right." The corners of his eyes crinkled, and I swam in their mossy green depths.

"It's not creepy I'm here?"

He shook his head. His smile stilled and slipped slightly. He took a small step closer. Tilting his head in silent question, he tucked his hands into his pockets. The fabric around his biceps stretched.

A blush warmed his cheeks.

My God, this man is too much.

"I could not be happier that you're in my room," he admitted.

A fleet of butterflies took flight in my gut, and I lost a brief battle with my face. I couldn't remember the last time I'd smiled that big. It felt like a warm summer breeze off the lakes back home. It felt like zooming down a hill on my bike with my hands off the handlebars. It felt like fireworks exploding across a navy sky.

I sank into the feeling. Empowered by it, I gripped his wrist, tugging him closer. He followed my urging. The hairs on my arms stood on end, anticipating another one of his all-consuming kisses. My legs ached to wrap around his waist. I eyed the hem of his shirt hanging loosely around his hips. Could I snake my fingers up and across his stomach?

One look at the lust in his hypnotizing eyes confirmed a resounding yes.

It didn't seem to matter what question my body asked his. The answer was yes. More.

"Why is it like this with you?" I whispered, hyperaware of the inches separating us. Barely room enough for words. The space filled with heat off his body, and the scent of his soap and minty toothpaste on his breath.

"I don't know. But I want it."

I took hold of the back of his neck and pulled his mouth to meet mine. Against my fingertips, the pulse in his wrist jumped.

The gates opened. The dam broke. I was flooded.

My heart thundered. Electricity sparked like lightning across my scalp and down my spine. There was no reason for restraint, and I gave in. All my impulses were safe. He confirmed it with the groan at the back of his throat, the hands that cupped my thighs placing me on the table, the scrape of his teeth along my jaw.

I hooked my ankles behind his back, the rock of my hips instinctual against the bulge behind his zipper. Impatience braided with desire in my veins. It was interminable. We'd just started—we'd just met—and already this was taking too long. He tasted too good. His fingers digging into my thighs, encouraging my movements was almost everything I wanted. His back flexed under my palms.

His tongue slid against mine. We both moaned as I sucked his lip. For a moment, we paused, staring into each other's eyes. I nodded, certain I saw a question there.

"I want all of this," I whispered.

"Tell me to stop if you change your mind." The words rushed from him as he closed the distance between our mouths again.

The hand at my thigh pressed higher, taking hold of my ass through my sensible slacks. It wasn't enough contact. The fabric was too thick, especially with his worn jeans dividing us as well. Reaching between us, I struggled with the button at the top of the denim.

He didn't relent. His lips continued down my throat. He tugged the neck of my sweater out of the way, revealing the white lace of my bra.

"You're all buttoned up, Lizzy." He licked and nibbled at the exposed curve of my breast. "It drives me fucking wild."

I tossed my head back, and he cupped my tits—his big hands overfilled with what I offered.

"Take off your pants," I commanded.

He glared down at the rise and fall of my cleavage against his fingertips before he took a step back. My clit throbbed, pleaded at the outline of his erection. I had to push my thighs together as he rubbed the heel of his hand up and down his length once.

"Pants off." This time it came out as more of a desperate request.

He ran the tip of his tongue over his already swollen lips. A disobedient glint sparked in his smoldering eyes. His biceps flexed against the white cotton as he lifted his arms and pulled his shirt over his head.

His wide ribcage expanded with each of his breaths. A pelt of dark hair curled across his rounded pecs. I didn't even realize I'd reached out to scrape my palm up his stomach until he closed his eyes, and his muscles twitched.

Standing, I put my mouth to his hot skin. Again, my fingers found his jeans' button, but this time I had the space I need to snap it open.

I slipped my fingers inside—the teeth of the zipper bit at the back of my hand.

He sucked in a sharp breath through clenched teeth as I gripped him. His hard length, thick and heavy against my palm.

A whine escaped from my throat when he took hold of my wrist, forcing me to let go of his cock.

He released me but tugged me flush to his body. His thigh pressed between mine. "Now you have too many clothes on."

I was in too much of a lust filled haze to realize he still hadn't given me what I asked for. I couldn't even understand how time worked. One moment I was fully dressed—if a bit sloppily—the next my slacks were undone and around my ankles.

He made a "Mmm" sound as he took hold of my thighs, his fingers dimpling into my flesh. "All buttoned up and pretty. It's been too much all night."

"Am I pretty unbuttoned?" I hardly recognized my voice and its breathy huskiness.

Shivers ran down my spine as he ran his hands up my sides to the row of buttons between my breasts. He pinched the top one, his dark green eyes bore into mine. The plastic disc slipped from the hole and my neckline sank deeper. "So much better than pretty."

His fingers lowered to the next button. Losing myself in the press of his mouth on mine, I slipped my arms free of my sleeves and pulled him tighter to my body. His jeans fell to his ankles. I gasped as his arms hooked under my ass and back. In one smooth movement, he lifted me off the table. I clung to his bunching shoulders. People did not generally pick me up—I was not a small person.

"I got you," he whispered in my ear for the second time that night.

He was so solid against me; I didn't doubt him. What was there to doubt? He was stability itself. In his arms, I was weightless. I surrendered to it. To everything.

To him.

Slow and easy, he lowered me to sit at the edge of the bed. He peeled my lace underwear down from my hips. On his knees, he licked his lips taking in the sight of my naked pussy. My chest caught on a shaky breath, the movement caught my attention in the mirror. I blinked in surprise at my own reflection. My hair was a mess, and my skin was flush. But I looked...incredible. Sexy. Empowered. Emboldened.

Burying his face between my legs, he tore a surprised gasp from me.

My eyes closed, and I fell back against the bed. The swells of my breasts barely held in by the lace of my bra.

I was lost in the sensations raging within the confines of my skin. How could I be merely human when he had me feeling like the stars were within my reach?

He hummed. The vibration sent me higher. His broad shoulders held my thighs open, his arms hooked around them. I must have opened my eyes, because the flex of his back between my legs forever seared into my mind.

His lips around my clit—he sucked and groaned.

Arching back, I cried out. Stars burst in my vision. I writhed and gripped the blanket under me into my fists. My orgasm racking through me.

I was still drawing in deep breaths when he sat back on his heels. The lower half of his face glistening. His usually bright eyes turned dark.

Jerking his head over his shoulder to the mirror, he asked, "Do you like watching?"

"I've never done it," I admitted.

My ability to understand and speak English in my state, deserved an award.

He pinched his lips together, running his palms up and down my inner thighs. I still felt the aftershock of my orgasm, as my body heated again.

"I really wanna watch us fuck in that mirror," he said, his desire barely restrained.

For half a moment, I worried it'd distract me. That instead of feeling all the ways our bodies gave pleasure, I'd see all the things that made me feel insecure. But then I remembered the version of myself I'd glimpsed just a few moments before.

"I want that too."

Muscles in his thighs, his stomach, but definitely in his thighs flexed as he stood. They were wide and long. The boxer briefs he wore stretched thin around them. His hard length strained against the stretchy material.

He loomed over me, his eyes as hungry for me as mine were for him.

A blush bloomed in my cheeks, as I lowered the band around his waist until his cock slipped free. It bounced in front of my mouth. I took hold of his base, thick and hot. Wetting my lips, I squirmed at his groan of equal parts anticipation and impatience.

He brushed my hair away from my face, taking hold of a handful at the roots.

I sighed, closing my eyes to his gentle pull.

He tugged my head back and waited for me to look up at him. "You like that?"

"Yes." I ran my hand up and down his length.

He sucked in a breath through his teeth.

"You like that?" I asked, knowing the answer.

He grinned down at me. "Behave."

That one word struck through me like electricity. I wanted to give it back, ratchet his need for me up the way he kept doing to me.

In one motion, I filled my mouth with his cock, sucking him to the back of my throat and moaning.

His hold of my hair pulled almost too tight. His hips jerked pushing his tip a bit further making tears sting my eyes. "Fuck," he ground out.

I took him in and out, swallowing him deeper each time. My cheeks hollowing. His ribs expanded with quick, shallow breaths. Rocking his hips, he fucked my mouth. My name a repeated plea and groan. He whispered dirty things about how perfect I looked with my lips stretched around him, and how he couldn't wait to fill my pussy.

I squeezed my legs together, needing pressure.

Without warning, he shifted away from me. One hand raked over his face, the other still holding tight to the strands of my hair. Slowly, his fingers loosened. He took a step back.

My head was light, and my blood rushed. My body was replaced with sparking energy barely contained within my skin. I needed release.

He tracked the movement of my hand as I swiped a bra strap off my shoulder and slipped my arm free. A muscle flexed in his jaw. When I lowered the second strap. The tight set of his jaw looked dangerous for his teeth. I reached my hands behind my back, undoing the clasps. I had to shake my tits from side-to-side to make the garment fall to my lap.

The growl that escaped his throat scraped down my spine, but it was the twitch of his hard cock that made me whimper.

In one quick movement, he hovered above me, forcing me back to the mattress again. He pulled one nipple into his mouth, sucking. I arched. My tit released from his lips with a pop, and he gave the same treatment to my other side.

Shifting back, he pressed kisses to my soft stomach. His big fists white knuckled on either side of my waist. His breath was humid puffs as he hissed, "You have me on the fucking edge."

He looked up from his brow to meet my eyes. "Stand up. Put your elbows on that table. Stick that goddamn glorious ass out."

I felt his commands in my core. Needy for more. Eager to follow his direction. But when he stood, I missed his weight. The distance between us was too much for my lust-soaked mind.

He swiped a hand down his face, searching. He spoke into his fist, "Condoms. Where are my fucking condoms?" Then he noticed me still on the bed and simply pointed a stern finger toward the mirror.

A slow smile spread across my face. "Bossy."

"Tell me you don't like it."

I pinched my lips together.

"If you're not where I told you to be by the time I find these fucking condoms."

Pushing myself to my feet, I stood.

The table was cold under my forearms. I turned my hips out, displaying my ass just like he wanted.

He searched through his duffle bag. After only a few seconds, wrappers crinkled behind me. I could tell the moment he turned around by the hiss of his breath—my ass up, my tits swollen, and my pussy wet and waiting.

Everything in the room went still. There was only the sound of my heart pumping inside of my ribs. Then the tearing of foil, the discarded condoms falling back to the floor, and the slip of fabric on skin. I craned my neck, taking in the view of Will naked. His erection curled toward his stomach, a drop of precum dripped from his tip, a bed of dark curls at his shaft's base. I ached to feel him push inside.

In his teeth, he tore the wrapper open. His strides closed the distance between us. He sheathed himself in the latex, taking his place behind me.

I had never been looked at like he looked at me. As if I was truly the most beautiful woman in the world. As if he wouldn't change anything about my appearance. As if to him I was perfect.

"You want this?" he asked. He cupped one of my ass cheeks and squeezed.

I sat back in his touch. "So badly."

Our bodies took over. I lifted to my tiptoes, and he bent at the knees. The head of his cock pressed against my entrance. He fit inside of me in one slow movement. Sinking deeper inch by inch, stretching me around his width until his hips sat against the curve of my ass.

I watched in the mirror as he took hold of my hips to keep me there, his arms flexed. He clung to me with more than his hands, as if he was searching for willpower and restraint.

"Will," I spoke his name, unable to express much else. Not when he was seated so deeply.

His grip tightened, and he eased out, then slipped back in. Over and over. He built up speed. The force of his skin hitting mine smacked and ricocheted through me. A cord strained in his throat. An unbridled desire as he gazed down at where we met.

I matched his pace. Begged for more. Cried out as he wrapped an arm around my hips, his rough fingertips finding my clit to rub circles.

He bit down on my shoulder, the bite of his teeth both grounding and what I needed to send me over the edge. My pussy spasmed around him, squeezing. He replaced his teeth with his lips as he twitched inside of me.

Our bodies were slick with sweat, but he stayed where he was, pinning me to the table.

He placed a kiss on the curve of my neck. His thighs were still firmly against my ass.

He met my gaze in the mirror, both of us stripped bare. Open and vulnerable.

"I can't believe I met you like this," he muttered.

"Me either."

"It can't just be tonight."

I giggled. "No, it can't."

Fifteen

Will

FOUR NIGHTS BEFORE CHRISTMAS

Lizzy, Rose, and I piled out of the rental car in front of a house with a large front porch and an attached garage. It had a tall gabled roof with dormers. Simple construction circa the 1940s, but it was well maintained and sat across the driveway from an enormous barn.

The wind bit frozen teeth at our cheeks and whipped at our coats.

Lizzy shrugged her shoulders toward her ears. Her hair blowing across her face.

"You cold?" I asked. "Do you want my hat?"

"No, I'll be fine." She jerked her head toward the barn. "It'll be warmer in the arena."

It took us a few more strides before we realized Rose had stopped. She shook her head and glared at me. "I'm going to need you to remember that you're *supposed* to be *my* boyfriend."

"Shit, right." As an afterthought, I added, "Do you want my hat?"

She turned to Lizzy, her eyes wide. "What did you *do* to him? He's, like, fully lost his mind."

Lizzy's face broke into a shy smile. If I hadn't already lost my mind, the dimple pressed into her cheek would have sent it on its way.

Cringing, I begged, "Be cool."

"You first," Rose demanded.

Avoiding a patch of ice, Lizzy started walking again. "Let's get inside it's freezing."

Stepping through the door, I let it slam behind me. It was warmer, not exactly comfortable, but the bitter wind couldn't snap at us anymore. The building was lit by rows of florescent lights. The smell of dirt and animal mixed in an almost pleasant way. At the far wall, stairs lead to an overlooking catwalk and offices. The dirt covered floor was mostly open, with only a sidewalk's width from the fence to the wall.

Rose narrowed her eyes, searching the face of a man speaking to a group of high school aged kids huddled together. He had at least some of their attention. His hands pushed deep into his pockets. "Is that Jack Brooks?"

"It is." Lizzy nodded.

Tilting her head, wrinkles creased Rose's forehead. "He looks different."

"He got a makeover for the bachelor auction a couple of months ago."

Rose's jaw dropped. "Bachelor auction?"

"It was so fun!" Lizzy's eyes glinted.

I couldn't help smiling at the two of them.

"Who is that?" Rose asked, her eyebrows shooting upward.

A man easily a few inches taller than my six foot one loomed to the right of Jack.

"That's Remi. He moved here to work at the animal clinic. Brooks works there too. Do you remember Hazel Matthews?"

"Nerdy girl, frizzy brown hair?"

"That's her. She bought the clinic from Doc March."

"Oh cool, good for her."

"Then she bagged Elijah March."

"No shit!"

"Yes!" Lizzy's eyes were bright as she passed on the gossip. "It's really freakin' adorable. He is so into her."

"Aw, well that's just cute." Rose pursed her lips to one side, before asking, "Is he still like..." She lifted her eyebrows.

"Oh yeah. The man has aged well."

"I'm still right here," I pointed out.

"Don't worry, you're pretty too," Rose joked.

"So pretty," Lizzy whispered to her boots.

I wouldn't say I *liked* being called pretty, but when it came from Lizzy...

A door on the second story opened and shut. A man in worn jeans, and a flannel waved down to us. He was obviously their cousin on their dad's side. He could have been a younger, slightly smaller version of Jim. "Horses are in the stables. Give me ten minutes. I'll be right down. Glad to see ya, Bud."

"You too," Rose called back, then she and Lizzy led me back to the freezing outside and into a different building. Wooden stalls with hay covering their floors lined the walls, most of them containing a horse. Just like every other time I'd come near one, I did not like their size.

We spent most of the day in the arena. The girls rode a couple of different horses to give the giant beasts exercise. My heart stuck in my throat each time either of them guided over a jump, kicking up patches of the dirt floor. They'd offered to help me ride. I'd almost said yes to Lizzy. Each time I shook my head, enjoying the feeling of my feet on the ground.

She did convince me to brush her mare before she led her to the stables.

"Like this?" I asked, more focused on the rise and fall of her breasts than my actual task.

"Not like that." She rounded under the horse's neck and placed a hand on mine. We froze, the sensation of her skin hot on my fingers. Her body was close enough that I could smell her sweet sweat over the scent of horse and dirt. My eyes followed her flannel covered arm to her face. Our mouths were inches apart.

The distance was dangerous.

She swallowed.

My blood rushed low.

"Like this," she directed, a little breathless.

It wasn't until she pulled her hand back and swiped it over her ponytail that I regained the presence of mind to glance around. Luckily, only Rose was positioned to see us, with an annoyed pinch of her lips.

I mouthed, *Sorry*.

She rolled her eyes.

I did a better job avoiding Lizzy after that.

Before we left, Rose, and I posed for a photo with one of the horses. It stood perfectly still, with its head between our shoulders. But I couldn't shake the fear that it might do something sketchy. It was just too big.

Lizzy lowered Rose's phone from in front of her face. "Will, you're glaring at Milkshake."

I leaned further away from the gargantuan animal. "It's called Milkshake?"

"How else would the boys get to the yard?" Rose asked.

She and Lizzy gave a sarcastic, "Duh," in unison.

Milkshake blew a gust of breath through its nostrils, and I jumped about three feet in the air.

"Let's get her away from him. She doesn't deserve this," Lizzy suggested.

I took a few steps sideways. "It's to my back. I can't relax."

"She, not it's," Rose corrected. Sharing an irritated look with Lizzy. "Go over by the fence next to the saddle. I'll be right there."

She made a clicking sound at the back of her teeth and began leading the mare away. My muscles were wound tight, but as the distance grew between me and *Milkshake*, my heart rate lowered. I rolled my shoulders and neck.

Lizzy tilted her head, considering me. "I didn't realize you were scared of horses."

"I'm not scared. I just don't trust them."

"Hmm. Important distinction."

I scoffed. "They're too big."

"Did you have any fun today?"

"Some. I liked watching you." I lowered my voice just above a whisper.

"I might have been showing off a little."

Denying the desire to hold her, to kiss her smirking lips, to tell her that the more I got to know her, the harder I fell was like denying that water was wet. She was right there, but completely out of my reach.

And I only had myself to blame.

"Alright," Rose called as she stepped back into the arena. "Let's get this photo and head home."

Sixteen

Lizzy

FOUR NIGHTS BEFORE CHRISTMAS

"Thanks for letting us ride," I said, bumping my cousin Emmett with my shoulder.

"Sure, anytime." He squinted toward Rose and Will, talking and laughing as they strolled to the exit. "What do you think of him?"

My expression remained neutral, even though I was hyper-aware that they had zero chemistry. They acted more like siblings than romantic partners. It was clear that they enjoyed each other's company, but it did not seem like they wanted to sleep together. With my hands tucked into my coat pockets, I shrugged. "He's nice. Why do you ask?"

"He doesn't seem weird with—" Emmett cut himself off to say instead, "to you?"

Did he actually say 'with'?

"He's been," I kicked a divot in the floor with the toe of my boot, "very nice. Good house guest. All of that."

"They just don't seem really into each other."

I was still struggling to think over the anxious voices in my head as he continued, "But then, maybe this is healthier for her."

"Than the way she is with Lawrence?"

Emmett nodded. Only a couple of years older than me and Rose, he'd always been much more observant and mature. It wasn't surprising that he'd noticed the dynamic between her and Will, or between me and Will.

"It's probably good that she and this new boyfriend are obviously...friends."

"Friends can become more, right?" It was as close to convincing as I could muster.

"I guess so. It just usually happens before they start dating."

The pit of my stomach grew heavy. It was one thing to lie to my parents. They didn't seem suspicious, but Emmett had always looked out for me. When people turned mean back when Rose and I had our falling out, he stood up for me. And throughout the entire day, he hadn't mentioned that it was strange for the two of us to hang out.

I sighed, hating the words I had to say next. Not just because he was my favorite cousin, but also because not so deep down—kinda right at the surface—I wanted Will for myself.

"Rose and Lawrence...are intense."

Emmett lifted an eyebrow.

I went on, beginning to see parallel lines between their situation and mine. "When they're in the same room, it's like they can't tell anyone else is even there. But she's not manic with Will. I think you're right. I think it is healthier."

"I hope so. Anyway, you liking him speaks highly."

The weight in my stomach turned leaden.

He glanced around the empty arena. The only other person in the building was his business partner, Missy. But she was up in her office with the door closed. "I know a lot of people are over Lawrence and Rose's drama—"

"—Mostly Shay," I interrupted.

A rare smile split his lips. "Mostly Shay. But I've always rooted for them."

My eyebrows pinched together. "Are you a romantic?"

"Does that make me one?"

"It might."

He lifted his shoulders and let them fall. "Then maybe."

❧❦

Rocking Around the Christmas Tree carried through the closed doors of the KC Hall. A group of my parents' employees stood huddled just outside, smoke and steam around their mouths glowing red from their cigarettes. The smell of nicotine burned in the frosty night. I jerked my head in hello before snaking inside the warm building. With a shiver, I shrugged out of my coat in the coat room and hung it on a wooden hanger that was probably older than me. I had to really throw my shoulder into parting everyone else's winter wear to make room for mine to fit.

My palms ran over the soft wool of my ugly Christmas sweater. Shay had made it required attire for the office party—considering I'd just walked past a man with the words 'I'd Rather be Wearing a Welding Mask' knitted across his chest, I thought she was on to something.

Just like at home and the shop, Mom had pulled no punches on the decorating. Unlike home, she'd skipped the traditional cozy feel and gone for a 70s look. Complete with a white tree decked in red garland and lights with shiny silver bulbs. The only green in the ban-quiet hall was on the sweaters worn by the attendees. The room was lit in technicolor from the twinkle lights blanketing the drop ceiling. In the corner, there were perfectly wrapped presents topped with extravagant bows. She'd even constructed a temporary fireplace with a television playing a burning log mounted inside of it. Another TV hung above the bar playing *Prancer*. Mom always claimed it was mine and Rose's favorite, but it didn't explain her obsession with the movie.

I rolled my eyes as affection warmed my chest. At least Mom still loved her work.

My gaze tugged to my left, landing on Will, as if compelled. Was it possible that I'd felt the pull of his eyes on me? That from across a dark room full of people, I'd been drawn to the heat of his stare?

Everyone else faded, the music quieted, until it was just us.

It was a pale comparison to the greeting I wanted—this prolonged eye contact. My heart swelled and broke all at once. In a few days, he'd leave, and I wouldn't have to resist my feelings any longer. But in its place would be his absence.

I wasn't sure which was worse.

"Hey girl." Shay bumped me with her elbow, popping the bubble.

I blinked, my mouth hanging open, gathering myself. "Uh, hi."

She took in Will, standing next to Rose, his arm wrapped around her waist. My cheeks burned.

Apprehension filled the dark pools of Shay's eyes, and something else that looked a lot like pity. "You're still about that? Even with all the red flags?"

"There are a lot of green flags, too." There was no denying my argument was pathetic.

She pursed her lips.

"I know you don't like it," I said.

"No, I don't."

I tugged on the neck of my sweater, feeling entirely too hot. "There's just something there. It's...new to me."

It was the biggest understatement. As if the pull between the two of us was because of how fresh it was.

What if it is? I swallowed, ignoring that nagging voice.

"Fine." She pointed toward the buffet table. "You hungry? The charcuterie board is my romantic interest tonight."

I grinned, grateful she'd let me off the hook for now. "Food would be great. We went to Emmett's today, and I kinda forgot to eat."

"Mm," she took a step, her heeled boot clipping on the floor, "how's my future husband doing?"

I scoffed. The list of men she planned to marry was long—not as long as the list of men she'd rather never see again. But my beloved cousin was not her one true love or anything.

I glanced around, ensuring that we were the only two people near the food table. "He's annoyingly observant."

"He saw through the whole thing?"

"Maybe." Perusing the spread of cured meats, fruits, and crackers, I grabbed a plate from the stack. "I think I smoothed it over for them, though."

"That must be weird, with how you feel about *him*."

"It's no big deal."

"Right," she said, the word dripping with sarcasm. Her focus moved past my shoulder, and she groaned. "Will you excuse me? I need to remind Lawrence to blink when he stares at your sister."

It didn't take me long to spot Lawrence sitting on a bar stool, with one boot propped on the rung. He was amongst his socializing coworkers. But his eyes were, in fact, trained across the room where Rose stood with Will at her side.

The longing etched into Lawrence's features—his covetous gaze, the tight set of his jaw, the pinch between his eyebrows—felt like he'd held up a mirror for me to peer into.

It had always scared me how consumed Rose and Lawrence were with one another. My emotions for Will were stronger than I'd felt for anyone else. I had to believe that we could be different. We could burn without exploding, without decimating ourselves and singeing everyone around us.

Seventeen

Lizzy

FOUR NIGHTS BEFORE CHRISTMAS

Even if the white wine glass in Mom's hand wasn't there, I would have been able to tell she had drank a couple by the pink in her cheeks. The sour smell of it was on her breath as she gave me a one-armed hug. Lowering to the metal chair next to me, she crossed her legs. "Hi, baby."

"Hi, Mom." I gestured to the room with a chocolate-covered strawberry. "You transformed the KC Hall, yet again."

She lifted her chin. "It's a skill."

"It really is. Having fun?"

"I always have such a good time at these parties." A couple of her words slurred together. It didn't happen often, but she was a sloppy and happy drunk. "What about you?"

"I haven't been here that long, and I'm driving, so I'll probably keep it to one drink." I pointed to my half full white wine.

"Your dad and I can give you a ride home."

"If that ice storm rolls in early tomorrow, I don't want my car stuck here."

"Oh baby, it's not coming for another 48-hours. And who cares if your car is here? It's no big deal."

"They'll have to plow the parking lot. I don't want it to get buried."

She stacked a cracker with Parmesan cheese and salami from my plate. "You worry too much."

"You're right, I'll just stop that."

"Good." Plopping the cracker in her mouth, she considered me. After swallowing, she said, "You and Rose are spending more time together."

I didn't want to get hers, or my, hopes up, not when I knew how badly she wanted us to be best friends again. But I had to face the possibility that Rose might go back to Kansas City and not talk to me again until Thanksgiving. So I gave Mom a noncommittal shrug.

She narrowed her eyes. "What do you think of Will?"

That I'm entirely too into him.

Hell, earlier today, I'd swooned like a regency romance heroine who'd never touched a man. All because he'd helped me *brush a horse.* I had traced a scar cut through the knuckle on his third finger. The white line was stark against his work-worn skin. When, in fact, I'd already had Will inside of me. I'd moaned and begged, wanton and hungry.

I found him at Rose's side. Our eyes met—we blinked and looked away.

"He seems really nice." My voice came out a little too high. I cleared my throat. "What do you think?"

"He's a nice man..." she turned her head toward Lawrence still nursing a beer and stealing glances of Rose. "I wish she wouldn't flaunt him in front of Lawrence, though."

My chair creaked as I sat up straight. "*Flaunt* him? That's a bit much. Is she supposed to not let her boyfriend touch her to spare her ex's feelings? Which he might not feel anything about."

He did. He definitely did, but that wasn't the point.

It was strange to defend my sister's right to receive the affection I desperately wished was for me.

"You know what I mean."

"I don't."

"I feel bad for Lawrence. He's been pining for her for so long, and she just floats in and out of his life."

Rubbing circles at the joint of my jaw, I exhaled before saying, "He is responsible for himself."

"Feelings get complicated."

"Doesn't change anything."

"You've always been so practical, and sometimes romance isn't practical."

"Mom, I have experienced romance."

"But have you ever been swept away?"

I groaned and rolled my eyes, which made her groan and roll her eyes.

"Some day, Lizzy, I hope you know what it is to be overpowered by your feelings for someone. To be *illogical* for someone."

Oh, the irony.

She turned her face to the ceiling as if she might find patience to deal with me up there. "Your sister might not be doing anything wrong, but she hasn't been doing the right thing by him for a while."

She'd uttered some version of these words throughout the years. The worst part was, I did understand her point. But the only people who knew the complete story were Rose and Lawrence, so who were we to judge?

"It's none of your business, Mom."

"I'm not saying it is." She held her hands up, one palm out, her other hand still held her wine, the contents sloshing dangerously close to the top. "I'm just saying that I empathize with Lawry."

"I think you're being unfair. He's just as responsible as she is."

"I never said he wasn't."

"But you feel bad for him? But not for her?"

"How do you think your sister would feel if the roles were reversed?"

I spoke in hushed tones, my irritation making my words string tightly together. "I would think a little relieved."

"That's the stu—"she pinched her lips together before correcting herself"—silliest thing I've ever heard."

My mouth hung open for a moment. "Were you going to say stupid?"

"No," Mom cringed, "yes, but I caught myself."

I snorted.

I couldn't explain why it was funny, but we both started laughing. She asked how horseback riding went, and we left the subject of my sister and her love life alone.

❧ ☙

Mitchell Williams spotted me before I spotted him. Avoiding him had been my main extra-curricular in high school. I was clearly out of practice because he swung his heavy arm across my shoulders. Beer spilled from his plastic cup and barely missed the toe of my boot.

It was late enough in the night that voices had raised in volume, and everything was a bit funnier than it had been a few beers ago. I was still sober but enjoying myself. Or I had been about four seconds ago.

He spoke directly to my breasts. "Lizzy, you've got a hot kindergarten teacher thing goin'."

With as little enthusiasm as I felt, I said, "Crayons on sweaters really do it for you?"

His grin took on a lascivious edge. "When they're on you."

"Avert your gaze."

"You always have something smart to say."

"Wish I could say the same."

"I hear you're finally single."

"Single doesn't mean interested, Mitchell." I tried to shrug out from under his arm, but he pulled me in tighter.

I shot him my most haughty, threatening glare. Considering how often he'd been on the receiving end, he was impervious. If I had known it only took a boyfriend to keep Mitchell from acting like a jackass, I would have lied about having one, too. "Get your arm off of me."

"We could be good, you know."

Will appeared in front of us. He had moved so quickly that I hadn't even noticed him coming. "Hey, man. I'm Will."

Mitchell tilted his head dumbly but didn't let me go to shake the hand extended to him. "I thought you were Bill."

"It's Will." There was a dangerous glint in his eyes, contrasting the big smile on his face. Under the tangled strings of Christmas lights, they appeared black. They darkened when he saw the frustration on my face. He jerked his still waiting hand. "You gonna leave me hanging?"

The pressure on my shoulders lifted, and I took one big step away. I was at equal parts relieved and irritated. What kind of bullshit was it that Mitchell would listen to a man, but not me?

Dick.

Shaking Will's hand, Mitchell introduced himself.

But when he went to retrieve his hand, Will didn't let go. His knuckles whitened from the force of his grip. His smile twisted into something menacing. With a voice lower and more threatening than I would have thought he was capable of, he said, "You're gonna keep this paw off of her."

I decided the thrill his protectiveness sent through me didn't deserve criticism.

"The fuck?" Mitchell pulled at his hand again. He was a little shorter than Will, and I could see Mitchell assessing the outcome of a physical fight. It didn't look good for him.

"Don't touch her again."

"What are you gonna do about it?"

"Why does he have to do anything?" I demanded, my arms crossed. "I want you to leave me alone."

Mitchell opened his mouth, but I cut him off, "Look, I'm your bosses' daughter. They wouldn't like to hear about this. You wanna keep your job?"

"That's fucked up."

I had to force my words through clenched teeth. "What's fucked up is ignoring what a woman wants."

He looked like he wanted to call me a name or two, but took in the warning written into every inch of Will—his weight on the balls of his feet, the bunch of his shoulders, and the watchfulness of his eyes. For the first time in his life, Mitchell did the smart thing and moved back. His hand, finally freed from Will's grip, was red.

Will turned his profile to me, watching the other man retreat. A muscle flexed in his jaw, and I resisted the urge to kiss him there. I was more than capable of taking care of myself, but having him watch out for me... He was making it hard to manage how much I liked him and perpetuating his and Rose's story.

I ran my fingers through my hair. "Thanks."

He shook his head.

Crossing my arms, I tore my eyes from the stern set of his brow. "You know I would have handled him, right?"

"Of course. I didn't like the look on your face when he had you like that, though." He rocked back on his heels. "Is it okay that I intervened?"

I nodded. "It sped the process up."

We considered each other for a moment. There was so much distance between us, and I just wanted to close it. The yearning was a physical ache. A deprivation pressed into the cavities of my heart.

"I like your shirt," he finally said.

I grinned. "What a perfectly acceptable way to say that."

His eyebrows pinched together, but I shook my head. Glancing down at the red and green crayons stacked on top of each other to make a Christmas tree, I said, "Thank you. I love the snowflake push-pins."

"It's cute."

"I like yours too."

He grabbed the hem and looked down like he had forgotten what he was wearing. The sweater was knit to look like a red and green flannel with fake buttons and all. "It's pretty cool, right?"

I giggled. "Cool, that's the word I'd use."

"No?" He smiled his winsome smile, drawing me into his warmth. "Bill, right?"

I jumped, forgetting other people were nearby.

"That's me." Will's usual grin fit back onto his face, directing it toward one of my parents' supervisors. This time when he shook the man's hand, it was friendly and not at all like he might tear the stranger apart.

The man pointed the mouth of his beer toward Will. "You do good work."

"Thank you," he said, but he glanced my way.

It's okay, I mouthed, taking a step back and turning. Behind me, I heard the man say, "There was a tray ceiling you did a couple months ago. Great truss work."

I'd seen people in town chat with Rose about the show over the past couple of years, but I had figured it was because she was from here. To see the excitement on people's faces to talk to Will, a stranger, was a little off-putting.

Mariah Carey sang *All I Want for Christmas* through the speakers, and I sighed wondering if it was possible for me to reserve a little part of Will for myself when everyone wanted his Bill persona too.

Eighteen

Will

Four nights before Christmas

"Is it true you might get on Netflix or something?" the man asked. I still hadn't gotten his name. But we'd talked about roof trusses at length. The whole time, I kept Lizzy in my peripheral vision.

The moment she'd arrived, she'd been a menace to my focus. With her navy pants following the curve of her hips and thighs. Her sweater accentuating her fullness. Even from a distance, I liked the way she moved. It wasn't necessarily graceful, but it was purposeful. There was an assuredness and efficiency to her steps. And those smiles that I'd fallen so hard for did not get handed out easily—making them that much more precious.

When that dickhead had touched her, I'd struggled with a nagging jealousy. I had no right to dislike anyone talking to her. Not while stapled to Rose's side, pretending to be a dutiful boyfriend. Lizzy's irritated expression had propelled me without so much as an, 'I'll be right back.' My vision turned red when she'd tried getting out from under his arm.

Watching her from afar, I grappled between only wanting to be with her and knowing that was the last place I should be.

"Somthin' like that." I'd emailed our agent, Elise, reporting our recent jump in followers a few hours ago, but I hadn't gotten a response yet.

"So how did you two get started?"

"Rose and I worked for the same builder, and neither of us liked the way he was doing things, so we bought a house and flipped it. She recorded the whole thing, and it's been going ever since," I explained.

"Oh, no, I know that from the show. I meant, how did you two start dating? Did you ask her?"

"Uh…"

Oh shit. How did we not discuss this question?

"It wasn't…You know…It just kinda happened," I stammered. "I think she asked me."

A crease formed between his brows.

I opened my mouth to stammer a better story when Lizzy strolled to the front hallway. Fear that she might leave gripped me, and my need to be near her grew too strong to fight. It overwhelmed all my thoughts. Just one more…I didn't know what would satisfy me.

"Will you excuse me?" I asked, but I was already walking away.

Taking long strides, I made my way to Lizzy with the stealth of an old spy movie—shoulders hunched, and glancing from side-to-side.

I turned into the coat closet and found her pushing her arm through her sleeve. The soft purple color deepened the brown of her eyes, bringing out the gold. Her hair cascaded in waves. The tether I held on to my resistance broke somewhere within the part of her lips.

I had just enough presence of mind to search for a door to close.

Some semblances of privacy. There wasn't one. But the racks sat fur-ther from the walls than was necessary. Just enough room. Probably.

Looking over my shoulder, I checked for anyone within sight. I put a hand on her hip. Her palms pressed to my chest. Her softly floral scent tickled at the back of my brain and woke something primal. I needed her pressed between me and the wall. I needed to run my hands up her curves. I needed her mouth on mine.

The hangers clattered together as I shoved my shoulder between them, creating an opening wide enough to fit behind them. She hur-ried between the fabric, and I followed. For a moment, we froze, suspended in time. On the other side, the party continued. Noise. People.

But in our makeshift hiding spot, it was just us.

"It's a bad idea," she whispered, understanding my purpose without explanation.

"It is," I agreed, but her mouth on mine swallowed my words.

I bit back a groan. She wrapped her arms around my shoulders. One of her hands raked through my hair. I leveraged her tighter to the wall, holding onto her soft waist. The desire to drive our forbidden kiss deeper was a deafening thunder throughout my body. Her head fell back as I ground my hips into hers, my erection seeking her warmth.

She tasted even better than I remembered.

How could a memory fade in only a few days? Especially as I clung to it, as if it might have saved me from a breaking point just like this.

I pinched her bottom lip between my teeth, and then let it slip gently free.

It wasn't enough. It couldn't be. It was a drop in a desert when I was dying of thirst.

Her breaths wracked through my chest.

I took in the garments hiding us. Regret turned just below my ribs.

How could I protect her if we got caught? She deserved so much better than this.

"I want more," she said, barely loud enough to hear.

"I want to give you more." I hoped she could see the truth of those words. That the word 'more' could be replaced with 'everything.'

Pressing my forehead to hers, I struggled with my shame. "I'm sorry, Lizzy."

"I...understand." Her acceptance brought me even lower—I would be underground soon.

I took in her swollen lips and the pink smear of her lipstick. Before I could change my mind, I took a step away. "You should leave first."

She tilted her head. For a moment, it looked like she might pull me back. And God knew I wouldn't resist her. But she slipped out, leaving me to pull upon every ounce of willpower I had not to follow her.

The coats swung on their hangers, and I wrestled with the possibility that I was making a huge mistake. Lying about my relationship with Rose might land us a streaming deal. But it could also cost me a chance with Lizzy.

❧❧❧ ❧❧❧

The clock in Rose's, and my bedroom continued to tick. Before she'd fallen asleep in the bed, she'd whispered, "I think you'd be good for Anne."

After a half-second to remember that Anne was Lizzy, I asked with too much enthusiasm, "Why do you say that?"

"Well, I *know* she'd be good for you. She'd help you plan better and be less spontaneous. Which obviously isn't a bad thing, but there's an argument that you and I could be more thoughtful."

"You mean like, not pretending to be your boyfriend for Internet clout?"

"Perfect example."

I grinned up at the ceiling. "Why would I be good for her, though?"

"You're loyal, and honest. And Anne deserves someone who is...captivated by her."

I was. She'd trapped me and I just wanted more of her captivity.

I swallowed, preparing myself. "I kissed her tonight."

"You did what?" Rose sat up in the bed to glare down at me.

"Yeah, I know. I'm a jackass."

"Yes, absolutely. But did she kiss you back?"

I thought of her fingers in my hair and her hungry mouth on mine. "Yeah."

"Wow." She fell back onto her pillow. "I might be wrong. You might be a terrible influence on her."

"Do you actually think that?"

"No, but you really are being a jackass."

I didn't bother to argue.

Rose fell asleep shortly afterward. I'd spent an unknown amount of time with my eyes closed, counting my breaths, praying for sleep. But it wouldn't come.

It was growing increasingly difficult in the quiet hours of the night to resist the urge to find Lizzy. To tap quietly on her closed door. To wait with held breath for her to allow me into her room. Praying to go unnoticed.

It was reckless. Getting caught fooling around with Lizzy would be immature at best. Her parents would never forgive me. It might salvage the situation if Rose and I came clean with her parents, but it wouldn't endear them to me. And my long game was to date Lizzy, to get to know her. Although we didn't need their approval, it would help.

There was something right between Lizzy and me. Even if wanting her was sweet torture.

I knew the taste of her, the way she gasped at my touch. She was everything I craved. Needing her was in my veins like fire. There was no putting it out. I just had to withstand it.

I could.

I would.

But I found myself throwing the covers off my torso and pushing to stand.

On bare feet, I padded out of the bedroom into the hallway.

Go back. You've already fucked up once today. Don't push your luck, the wiser part of my brain urged. I didn't listen.

The wood floors were cold on the soles of my feet. I stepped as quietly as manageable. My heartbeat like thunder shaking the earth. Every breath boomed down the quiet hall. It was in my head. I knew that. But just like I knew it was a terrible idea to stand outside of her door, I paused anyway.

Pressing my ear to the wood, I tapped twice with my fingertips. Waited.

Nothing.

She was probably sleeping. I should be too.

Go back to your room.

I'd dodged a disaster of my making. No one had seen me outside of her room like a desperately horny teenager. The possibility of a future with Lizzy hadn't imploded in my face. Really, it was only a few more days of staying under the same roof and then there'd be...so much space between us. States upon states between us—a quarter of a large country.

I missed her already. The feeling unjustified and confusing. If having her this close and out of touch was torture, the concept of so much distance was definitely worse.

I continued down the hall toward the dim light over the kitchen sink. Less careful to be silent, I opened a couple of cupboards, searching for a cup. I filled it and clung to the cold glass like it was a grip on my sanity. Lifting it to my mouth, I considered tossing it in my face. Something to break me out of this daze. Life was out of focus and hazy, and she was in vivid detail. The red and gold strands amongst the brown of her hair. The gentle press of her clavicles against her skin. The dimples at the base of her spine hidden under her clothes.

Running a hand down my face, I begged to a higher power for strength as I downed the glass of water in thirsty gulps.

I braced my hands on either side of the sink, glowering at my reflection in the window above it.

My smarter half was about to win out when an uncorked bottle of red wine on the counter caught my attention. From behind the basement door came muffled Christmas music.

Even my smarter self fell quiet.

Lizzy

Four nights before Christmas

A slice of dim light cut down the stairs when Will opened the basement door. I knew it was him, like I knew the thrum of my pulse. My fingers tingled, remembering the strands of his hair between them, the press of his powerful body. I was foolish when it came to him—If we'd been caught making out behind coats...I wouldn't survive the humiliation. I couldn't find it in me to care.

Not when leaving him had felt like deprivation.

My aching need grew with every detail I learned about him. He'd been so sweet in the car on the way to the stable, maneuvering the conversation to include me and Rose. Asking us questions about our favorite Christmas gifts, we had the same answer: a trip to Hawaii for our senior year spring break. We'd talked over each other, recalling hiking to waterfalls, and snorkeling, and laughing at our dad discovering he loved fresh ocean fish. Both of us doing our best impression of him repeating, "This is ridiculous."

Will's favorite gift was from his mom, his childhood dog, Scout. "She was a good dog," he'd said, his voice etched with reminiscence.

He had a comfort with vulnerability that most people struggled with—me included. But in the presence of his openness, I found my guard dropping—allowing the shattered pieces of my heart to fit back together.

And then the way he'd swooped in and handled Mitchell. Will's protective side was just as sexy as every other angle I'd seen of him.

"Hello," he whispered from the top of the stairs.

"Hi," I whispered back.

I barely heard him close the door over the softly playing music. His descent was near silent. Each step punctuated my anticipation, amping up my excitement.

We were alone.

Finally.

Taking the last step, he planted his feet shoulder width apart. His white T-shirt was loose around his waist but fitted to his shoulders and pecs. His gray sweatpants sat low on his hips. He looked perfectly confident, except for his bare toes curling and uncurling on the carpet.

With the tilt of his head, he lifted the wine bottle I'd left upstairs. "Can I top you off?"

I resisted the corny urge to answer, *I thought you'd never ask*. Instead, I nodded and lifted my nearly empty glass.

"What are you doing down here in the dark?" he asked.

I jerked my head toward the laptop open on my lap. "Working."

Heat burned my cheeks as I realized that was what I intended, but I was actually scrolling through his Instagram. It'd lured me like a moth to the flame when I'd gone to the show's profile. The top post was the picture I'd taken earlier of him and Rose. In it he was looking at, or possibly just past, the camera with an intensity I recognized.

The top comment was from @iliketodoitmyself saying, ***If Bill looked at me the way he's looking at the camera I would combust.***

Girl, same, I thought, but I didn't respond.

I sat my glass on the side table, angling my computer away from Will. Judging by his lifted eyebrow, I didn't angle far enough.

"Is that me?" He leaned down, putting a hand on the back of the sofa, the knuckle of his thumb touching my shoulder. That one point of contact was enough for my heart rate to jump. My lungs wanted more air, but I was sure he'd notice if I started panting.

"It's pro bono work," I lied.

He lifted a skeptical eyebrow.

"Your social media presence is the bedrock of your advertisement efforts. Should you ever suffer from scandal or a change in algorithm, it'd be wise to establish a few other avenues to drive business."

He straightened and grinned down at me. "Nice save."

"Thank you." I closed the laptop and set it down on the coffee table.

"Have more thoughts?"

"Always."

The sofa was old and beaten in, and I sank a bit in his direction when he lowered onto the opposite cushion. I propped my elbow to rest my chin. I was overly aware of the space he took up, the negative space that I could fit into. My sudden lack of confidence caught me off guard. Just a few hours ago, I'd been willing to risk it all for the quickest make-out session in a coat closet.

"Here." Will patted his thigh.

"You want me to sit on your lap?"

He cocked his head to the side as if to say, *Kinda.* But what he said was, "Prop your feet on me so you don't have to be all corkscrew."

My pulse lost a beat or two. A fresh surge of energy lit me up from the inside. I was going to get to geek out about one of my favorite things, while touching him without having to pretend it was an accident or hiding.

I rotated, setting my bare feet on his firm thigh. One of his big hands circled my ankle, and it took me a moment to recover.

"What were you saying about algorithms?" he asked, running his thumb from the top of my foot to the bottom of my calf.

I swallowed. "Um...A better place to start would be, how much of your finances are based on your flips and how much is based on your YouTube channel?"

A crease formed between his eyebrows. "It's still primarily flips. I'd say 75-25."

"Okay, so a significant amount from the show. One benefit of it is that it's evergreen material. Even if details of a video fall out of fashion, there's still helpful information there. And obviously its residual income. But you also sacrifice privacy."

His hold on me tightened, then relaxed. "Would that be a problem for you?"

"No, it's no problem to create an infrastructure for your business. We just have to be strategic."

He bit his lower lip, his teeth glinted in the lights of the mini Christmas tree in the corner. "I meant, would it be a problem for *you?*"

"Oh." I pinched the hem of my sweatshirt between my fingers, folding it over and over. "It would...be challenging."

A muscle ticked in his jaw.

"But um..." I began reminding myself how rewarding being bold had been. "I would be willing to try."

His eyes flicked to mine. It was too dark to make out their color, but there was no missing the heat in them. "You would?"

"This is," I searched my mind for the right word, "complicated."

He scoffed.

"But it's given me a chance to see you, the way you help my sister, how genuinely kind you are. I like you."

He tilted his face away from me, hiding his expression. "You deserve better than this."

A million partial thoughts flitted through my mind, but they all agreed with him. At the same moment, I didn't feel used, just dissatisfied.

I finally said, "It's temporary."

I glanced down at my fidgeting fingers. "It'd take some finessing. You and Rose would announce your break-up"—I put finger quotes around break-up—"You and I could date in secret for a few months. I wouldn't want to go public because it's just not me."

"So, you wouldn't openly date me?"

"That's not what I'm saying." I wrapped my hands around my thighs and pulled myself closer to him. "I wouldn't want to be on your show, or on any of your social media. We'd be public in our lives, but not on the internet."

"Given some thought?"

If you only knew how much I think about you...

"Some," I conceded. "Would that be enough for you?"

"Yes." He answered without hesitation. There was something so earnestly sweet about it. I fell a little further for him.

I nodded.

His thumb went back to its up and down motion. I was robbed of my ability to think. There was still more to discuss. Long-distant relationships were hard, and I didn't know how it would work, but he had a way of keeping me in the present. At that moment, we had an opportunity I wanted to take advantage of.

"No one knows we're down here," I whispered.

He froze before his eyes drew searing lines up my legs and body. His eyes bore into mine.

"If anyone walked down the hallway," I continued, "we'd have enough warning."

He swallowed. His shoulders clenched. I wanted to run my hands over the bound muscles. To wrap my legs around him. To have his mouth on mine and end the deprivation.

It had only been a few days, but the memory of his body on mine, in mine, kept me awake at night with need. My pulse drummed a beat through my whole body.

His eyes flicked to the ceiling, then to me.

The graze of his fingertips up the thin layer of my leggings sent shivers down my spine.

He gripped the back of my knee. "We have to be quiet."

"I can be quiet," I promised.

The press of his lips on the inside of my knee burned through fabric. My back arched. My nails scraped against the sofa cushions. I gasped.

Already too sensitive to his touch. It would have been humiliating if I wasn't so incensed.

"Shhh." He breathed down my thigh.

He pushed my leg between his body and the backrest.

With every kiss he pressed to my stomach, my chest, my throat, bound my heart. Until he brushed his soft lips along my jaw.

I bit my lips between my teeth to keep from calling out.

Hooking my legs around his waist, I pulled his mouth to mine. The brush of his tongue pulled me from underwater. My lungs filled with air, my body desperate for the oxygen that only he could provide. The soothing clarity that he was just as needy for me. I couldn't explain how I knew. Whatever called from within me found its answer in him.

His fingers dug into my waist.

We both groaned as I rocked my hips. The pressure of his hard cock against my sensitive clit sent shivers down my spine.

A floorboard overhead creaked.

We stilled except for the rise and fall of our chests.

Twenty

Will

FOUR NIGHTS BEFORE CHRISTMAS

Lizzy looked thoroughly kissed, with her hair wild around her shoulders from my grip buried in the strands. We were breathing like we'd done thirty minutes of cardio. If whoever was moving above us in the hallway came downstairs, they'd know what she and I were up to.

It'd help if I peeled myself off her. But she felt too good. Soft. Full.

Unconsciously, I rocked my hips from side-to-side. My throbbing cock pressed against her was torture and relief all at the same time.

I gritted my teeth, fighting back a groan.

A whine escaped from her.

I shushed, but it would have been more convincing if we weren't silently laughing.

She tickled my ear, whispering, "That was your fault."

"I know."

She lifted her hips, and my eyes closed from the bliss of her heat through the thin fabric of our pants. The only sound was the rustle of our clothes as we held our breaths. I pressed a kiss to the pulse in her throat. It thrummed quick and urgent.

Overhead, the creaking of footsteps retreated before going silent.

I supported my weight on my elbow to look down at her. Her features cast in a multicolored glow from the twinkle lights on the miniature Christmas tree at the other end of the room. She'd been adorned in shadows since the first night I'd met her. A gentle drape of light on her eyelashes and cheeks. Round brown eyes that saw every detail, assessing everything.

She took me in now, a quirk to her lips. "What are you thinking?"

"You can't tell?"

Shaking her head, a smile spread across her face. "How could I?"

"I just figured it was written all over my face."

"What?"

"I like you so much."

She hid her face, pressing it to my chest. "I like you too."

My heart was going to break free from my ribs. It pulled to hers. Lowering, I rested it against the swell of her breasts. It wasn't close enough.

She peered up at me, her eyes darting between mine. "I've never had sex in this house."

I lifted an eyebrow. "No time like the present."

Her head fell back, silent laughter shaking her body. I caught a groan in the back of my throat. Just looking at her—the exposed skin of her neck, her hair swaying toward the floor, the bounce of her tits—was enough to make my cock twitch.

I urged her mouth to mine.

Red wine clung to her lips. I was drunk on the taste of it, of her. Her tongue slipped along mine. She wrapped her arms around my shoulders, pressing us tighter together. Her legs hooked around my hips, and I ground my aching erection against her.

In the silence, I noticed every shiver that ran through her body. Her gasp as I trailed kisses and little bites down her throat. The arch of her back when I snaked my free hand up her sweatshirt, cupping her breast over her bra. Her nipple puckered in my palm. She overfilled my grip—the heavy flesh spilling between my fingers. She was more than I could hold. And I had big hands.

"I want you," I whispered into the hot skin just above her heart.

"Yes," she moaned.

Sighing, I wished I'd thought this through. Story of my goddamn life. "I don't have a condom."

"I might."

My head jerked up. "Down here?"

Her teeth pressed into her lower lip.

"In my laptop bag." It was hard to tell in the dark, but there might have been a blush coloring her cheeks. She lifted one shoulder. "Can never be too prepared."

A smile spread on my face. "Never change."

She snorted.

I shushed. I was tumbling into emotions too big to whisper, with nothing to break my fall.

I pushed back to kneel. Lizzy's legs held tight, pulling her with me. She looked so good there. Disheveled and lustful. Her thick thighs spread. I ran my hands up them, squeezing into their softness. My needs conflicting my actions. Untangling from her was the last thing I *wanted* to do, but it was the only way to reach for the bag leaning against the coffee table.

The bag rustled, the metal jingling, when I picked it up and put it within her reach. With silent, deliberate movements, she lowered to the carpeted floor. Bending over the bag, put her perfect ass up for my appreciation. I didn't even question running my palm from one round cheek across to the other. She arched into my touch.

I took hold of the spandex clinging to her waist. Tugging it down, I exposed inch after inch of her skin.

Flipping her hair, she directed, "Only take them off one leg. In case we have to get dressed fast."

I was no better than a deranged Neanderthal because I hadn't even considered a strategy for putting clothes back on. How could I when her ass was bare? The waistband of her leggings rolled to her mid-thigh.

She wasn't wearing any underwear.

I slipped my fingers between her thighs, and I slid my middle finger inside of her. Her ribs expanded. She'd stopped looking in pockets of the bag, instead she fucked back into my hand.

"Did you find that condom?" I placed the pad of my thumb at the entrance of her ass. Precum darkened my sweatpants.

"I can't—your hand—I can't," she whimpered.

Although I loved her speechless at my touch, I ached to feel her stretched around my cock.

I pulled my hand from her heat. The sofa creaked as I sat back. I ran my hand down my face, smelling her on my fingers. My groan came out as a sigh. Wanting her was past urgent—she'd been edging me for days.

Turning, she held up a square foil. "Got it!"

"I need you." I wondered if she understood all the ways those three words were true. Before her, I didn't know what I was missing. But I did now. "Come here."

She crawled the few feet to kneel between my knees. I lifted my hips for her to lower my pants below my erection. It sprung free before settling curved toward my stomach. She moistened her bottom lip, and my balls tightened.

I hooked a finger under her chin. My heart paused, then pounded as she lifted her face. She was so beautiful. Everything fell away except for her. The ridge of her upper lip, and her eyelashes lining the loveliest eyes I'd ever seen.

I wanted to tell her, but I couldn't string my thoughts together.

I swiped my thumb along her cheek. "Just come here."

She swallowed and stood. I placed kisses on her hips and thighs as I helped her free one of her legs. With both of her hands braced on my shoulders, I read her grip like Morse code. Each little flinch told me where to kiss her next. Her hold tightened as I trailed down the crease of her pelvis until I could part her lips with my tongue and taste her arousal.

I urged her closer, putting more pressure on her clit. She cut off the moan that slipped from her mouth. It was what we'd agreed, but I missed hearing her. Since we couldn't, I'd make do with all the other ways we communicated. Like the way she rocked her hips when I slid two fingers inside of her again.

She squeezed tighter and tighter.

Lost in the taste of her, the feel of her hot and wet, it took me a moment to hear her gasping my name.

"Not like this," she whispered when I leaned back. "I want you inside me."

I licked her from my lips and ran a hand through my hair. A fog coated the layers of my mind, making everything but her incoherent. She was my entire perception. My world began and ended with her.

She rolled the condom down my shaft, and I bit the inside of my cheeks from the pressure. Straddling my thighs, she placed my tip at her entrance, then lowered slowly surrounding me. Her head fell back when she'd seated me inside of her. Before she could lift, I put my arms around her hips and pressed her lower, filling her until I felt her limit.

Her mouth fell open, but no sound came out.

I buried my face in her hair. "Is that too deep?" I whispered, rough as gravel.

She shook her head. A quiet, shuttered, "No. It's good. Really good."

Around my cock, she grew tighter. Gripping her hips for dear life, I urged her to take slow, deep strokes. I held on to my control with everything I had. The clench of my teeth. The bunch of my shoulders. My tenuous grasp on reality.

She held her breath. Her pussy squeezed. Tears clung to her eyelashes.

Cupping the back of her neck, I pulled her forehead to mine.

We moved together, our eyes locked. Nothing but the pounding of our hearts and our bodies urging for more. For everything.

By some miracle, she came first. Her core flexed and spasmed around my cock, and she shivered. She closed her eyes, twin tears traveled down her cheeks.

I followed, biting down on her sweatshirt to keep from making any sound. A shiver ran up my spine. Behind my eyelids, I saw lights dance and my head went light and empty.

It took a few moments to catch my breath.

She turned my face to kiss me. A tender press of her lips to mine. There was nothing but her and me. We were everything. And it was enough.

I knew this moment couldn't last forever. But I wanted it to.

Twenty-One

Will

THREE NIGHTS BEFORE CHRISTMAS

"Olivia is in town today. Is it cool if I spend some time with her?"

It took me a moment to realize Rose was speaking to me. I was too busy remembering Lizzy straddling my lap. Sinking down, taking me inside of her the night before to register much of anything else.

"My friend Olivia," Rose said. "She's in town for Christmas and I'd like to spend time with her. Will you be able to figure out something else to do today?"

The morning sun burned warm through the bay window at our backs. Her mom was typing loudly on her keyboard in the adjoining office. Somewhere in the house, Lizzy was working as well. I couldn't think of a good enough excuse to find her. I just wanted to be in the same room.

"Yeah, of course. Who is she again?" I tapped my fingers on the velvet sofa arm.

"The one with the shitty fiancé."

"Ah, right." I recalled Rose complaining about her friend's engage-
ment to a total asshole, but I wouldn't have recalled the person's name.

"Is he shitty?" Kelly asked over her persistent clicking.

"The worst."

"In what way?"

Rose arched an eyebrow. "Um...she doesn't *say* anything. You know
how she is. But the only good thing *I* can say about him is he's gainfully
employed, and hot."

"Well, that's sad. After everything she's been through..."

Rose nodded, even though her mom couldn't see her. "Is it okay if
I take the car?"

"Sure," I agreed. "I'll find something to do."

Fifteen minutes later, Rose and I exchanged an awkward hug after
she went to kiss me on the cheek, and I went for her forehead. Giving
up on salvaging the goodbye, she exited out the side door. The engine
of the rental car came to life, and Kelly called from the office, "Will can
you do me a favor?"

My stomach dropped, overwhelmed by a paranoid fear that her
next words were going to be along the lines, *"Can you* not *fuck around
with my daughter in the basement?"*

Forcing my expression calm, I leaned against the doorjamb. "What's
up?"

She grinned at me like the cat who ate the canary. "You get along
really well with Lizzy."

Cold sweat prickled across my skin.

"I've noticed," she went on more stiltedly, "that you're helping the
girls...reconnect."

"I don't know how much I play into that."

"I don't either, but I'm happy to see it, anyway."

I curled and uncurled my toes inside my comfortable socks. "So, what can I help you with?"

"I want you to take Lizzy shopping for a gift for Rose. She usually gets store credit somewhere, but it'd be nice if she got her something more personal. She just might not know what to get her, but you probably would."

"Uh, I'm not great at gifts, but I can try." Anxiety still twisted my gut, but relief was slowly untying the tension.

And that was the Christmas miracle that put me sitting in the passenger seat as Lizzy drove to a nearby mall—at her mom's request. Lizzy tapped the steering wheel, silencing the stereo as soon as the first note of a song began to play.

The waves of her ponytail swung as she looked both ways before pulling out of her driveway, and I remembered burying my fingers in the strands as I slipped inside of her.

I sucked in a sharp breath—the memory sparking echoing sensations through my body.

"Everything okay?" she asked.

"Mm-hm." I cut my eyes her way.

A devious grin split across her face, understanding the directions of my mind. "Oh, yeah. You're fine."

"What *have* you done to me?"

"Nothing you didn't deserve."

"We need to change the subject, or we're going to have to find somewhere to pull over."

"I didn't debauch you enough last night?" she purred.

"I'll never get enough of you."

Pink rose up her neck and filled her cheeks. Her lips pursed, struggling against a smile. She had a way of pulling at the strings of my heart, made it swell too big for my chest. It thudded against my ribs. I rubbed the heel of my hand into its persistent beat, but it wouldn't calm.

I jerked my chin toward the silent radio. "What were you listening to?"

She chewed her bottom lip. "Miley Cyrus."

"Why'd you turn it off?"

Wrinkles creased her forehead. "Um...I guess because my ex hated my music. So, I turned it off on reflex."

"I don't mind. *Party in the USA* is one of my go-to karaoke songs."

She snorted. "Of course."

"What? I listen to Miley?"

"Karaoke. Nightmare."

"To sing or just be there at all?"

"All the above."

"Would you just go and hangout with me?"

"Do you really like it?"

I shrugged. "I have a lot of fun."

She chewed her full lower lip. "I'd go. But only if you promise not to dedicate a song to me."

"I promise not to *tell* other people that I'm dedicating a song to you. But you'll know."

The smile she'd been fighting won out. "Fine."

It felt like more than a compromise about something pithy. It felt like common ground. It felt like there was space where I could be outgoing and ridiculous, and she could be prickly and quiet. There was room for both of us.

⁂

"We got all the way here, and I still don't know where to begin." Lizzy's voice echoed a bit in the mall's interior hallway, over the Christmas music.

"Gift shopping is like that, isn't it?" Jerking my head toward a bookstore, I grabbed her hand. "Let's just look around."

She trailed behind me through the open doors. The smell of coffee and baking cookies wafted in the air from the cafe to our right. Bookshelves covered the bulk of the floor space, but the music and game department were decent.

Lizzy paused to flip through a planner decorated in pastel colors and soft lines.

"Need a new planner?" I asked.

She shook her head. "No, I keep everything electronically. It's just pretty."

"Do you want it?"

"There's no point." She closed the cover and ran her hand over it. "I'd just own it to own it. I don't actually have a use for it."

I tilted my head, trying to get a better look at her face, to make sure I wasn't imagining the wistfulness in her voice. "Does everything have to have a purpose?"

"No, but planners should, I guess." She looked over her shoulder at the stacks of books. "Does she read much anymore?"

I allowed the change of subject. Shaking my head, I tried to remember if I'd ever seen Rose with a book in her hand. "I wouldn't say so."

"Hm, she used to."

"Do you read a lot?"

"As much as I can." There was a tone to her voice that brought me to a stop—a deep emotion barely restrained.

I turned to face her. She'd drawn in on herself going too still, just like she did that first night I met her. When she'd been nervous and without control. I tucked a lock of her hair behind her ear, wrapping my other arm around her waist. Giving her whatever comfort I could.

"You should get her the last book you liked."

Her lower lip slipped from between her teeth. "I don't know. Do you think she'd like it? Doesn't that seem like a, *I didn't know what to get you,* gift?"

"It seems like a way for her to get to know you again."

She looked more unsure than I'd ever seen her. Leaning forward, she rested her head on my chest, tucked perfectly under my chin. After a few breaths, she said in an unwavering voice. "I miss her."

Her temple was warm under my lips. "She misses you, too."

Just a few more beats passed before Lizzy straightened. "We should probably be more careful."

I wanted to pull her tight again, to tell her I didn't care. But my choices affected Rose too. I should have been more aware of my actions. I felt small, letting them both down in so many ways.

We should come clean. The thought sparked in my mind like the flip of a switch. The show and the fans be damned. But it wasn't a decision I could make on my own. Maybe Rose would at least consider telling her parents. It'd help to stop lying to them.

To be absolutely truthful with myself. With Lizzy.

Twenty-Two

Lizzy

THREE NIGHTS BEFORE CHRISTMAS

Will and I arrived home from shopping just before Rose. I hurried to my bedroom to stuff my bags into the closet. As soon as she stepped through the garaged door, she began flitting around the kitchen.

"I found this recipe for a Christmas sangria. I'm gonna throw it together. You want some?" she offered, her voice muffled from the other side of my wall.

"Should we get ready for the thing at the school?" Will asked.

"We have time. I could use a drink."

"Everything okay?"

"Yeah." She called out, "Anne, you want a glass?"

A smile split across my face. The delight of being included by her was still very real. I didn't have to tamper it when no one could see me. "Yes, please."

I stepped into the hallway to find Rose bright faced and energetic, a little frantic.

Will and I hovered around the kitchen island while Rose poured ingredients into a pitcher. He rubbed circles on my back, and I closed my eyes, savoring his touch, even if my parents could walk into the room at any moment. I wanted to live in the bubble where it was okay for us to be affectionate for a while longer.

After pouring three champagne flutes, Rose immediately lifted hers to her lips downing the contents then stared into space. I sent Will a questioning glance, but he just shrugged.

"I'm gonna go get ready." He placed a kiss at my temple before leaving.

I felt it in the safety of my rib cage. A seed that had been sowed and sprouted but was now beginning to bloom. My emotions were too tender. I wanted this too much. It would hurt too badly for it to fall apart.

Rose glanced down the hallway after the door closed behind him. "I assume Mom and Dad aren't home?"

"I don't think so."

Whatever veil was draped over her slipped away. Her eyes brightened with a mischievous glint. "So, you hung out with Bill?"

I bit my lower lip, looking down at the countertop. "Yeah, Mom sent us off Christmas shopping. Is that okay?"

"Why would you need my permission?"

I narrowed my eyes at her. "I don't wanna blow your cover."

She snorted. "It's cool. I want it to work out for you two."

"Thanks." A swirl of butterflies flitted around my heart. "Is he really as great as he seems?"

"He is."

"Why didn't you two..."

"You haven't noticed the lack of chemistry?"

I rolled my eyes. "I saw that kiss the other morning. Haunting. But like, why?"

"Bill and I are just not it, you know?" In one big gulp, she downed her beverage. "I seem to only have fuck buddies and platonic friendships."

"Recently?"

She nodded, staring down at her empty glass. "And not recently."

"Since?"

"Yup."

"There hasn't been anyone since Lawrence?"

She pinched her lips to one side. Raising an eyebrow, she shook her head.

Staring into the middle distance, misery seated in the corners of her eyes. "He was there today. In the group with Olivia."

"You, okay?"

Swallowing the remaining contents of her drink, she shrugged. "I don't know if I have been in a long time."

I wanted to hug her, but the new rules of our relationship were unclear. Instead, I uttered an impotent, *That sucks.*

I turned her words over. Realizing just how much Rose had lost over one decision she'd made when she was eighteen. Lawrence and I had been load-bearing pillars of her support system. To have both of us knocked out from underneath her must have left her crumbling. While I'd been swallowed by depression and fear at my first life experience alone. So had she. It'd just shown differently.

But we were both keeping the world at arm's length.

The question remained...

Could I break the pattern?

I'd pulled my hair into a headache inducing bun, and the woman sitting next to me in the high school auditorium wore a too sweet perfume. My sweater dress was hot and itchy around my neck as the students in the orchestra played an extra melancholy and poorly timed, *I'll be Home for Christmas.* I'd considered staying home, but our cousin Violet played the flute. So, just like all the other dutiful friends and family members, I waited for the concert to end.

We all filed into the cafeteria afterwards for juice from an Igloo cooler with a spout at the bottom and store-bought sugar cookies. They had strung red and green streamers and balloons along the brown brick walls. Rose and Will lingered next to the entrance talking but not looking at each other, as if they were characters in a spy movie scoping out the place. They really did have terrible chemistry. It was a shock that their fans were hungry for a relationship between them.

I might be biased. Or I knew what Will was like when he liked someone—instead of just being a good friend.

I followed my parents, waving hello to old classmates and former teachers, until we were standing next to Violet and her friends. A girl with dark curly hair widened her eyes as she registered my face. But I couldn't imagine why. I didn't think I knew her.

"You all did such a good job!" Mom wrapped her niece in a hug.

"Thank you," Violet said, in her usual distracted way. Ever since she was little, she'd had a spacey way about her.

Her friend scrolled on her phone, then paused and showed the screen to a tall blond girl. They both looked at me. I stilled to resist fidgeting from one foot to the other. I couldn't fathom how I had become the center of their attention, and I knew from being one, teenage girls were terrifying.

Dad threw an arm around Violet's shoulders. "It was good."

"Thanks, Uncle Jim."

"Hey," the first girl stepped toward me, "you're Rose's sister, right? Rose from *Will it Bloom? Renovations*"

"Uh, yeah."

"Are you like friends with Bill, too?"

Mom sent me a questioning look. I shrugged back, certain that my face was growing bright red. "Sure."

"Okay, 'cause I saw this adorable picture of you, and I was like, 'Oh my God, is he becoming besties with her sister too!' Like, could he be more perfect?"

My fingers tingled from adrenaline. In my chest, my heart pounded like a tiger was chasing me. "Picture?"

"I wouldn't call him *perfect*," Dad whispered to Mom, and she elbowed him in the ribs.

I opened my mouth to tell my dad he was wrong, but then the girl held her phone a few inches from my nose. The image was a blur of color and light until I leaned far enough away.

"Jeez, don't shove your phone in her face," the tall blond admonished.

"Sorry." The girl pulled her phone back a few inches, but I could make out the image. In it, I was mid eye roll and smiling. In my hands, I held a Christmas chessboard. And he looked at me with the warmest affection. So warm I could feel it through the phone.

The girl put a hand on her hip. "Some of the comments are dumb, like thinking that he's cheating on Rose with you. But I was all, '*She's her sister. Obviously, she and Will are friends.*'"

I didn't have enough saliva in my mouth to speak, not that I knew what to say, anyway. Jerking my head, I managed something like a nod.

"Well, now Rose will know you two went shopping for her," Mom said, shaking her head. "Is that the gift you got her?"

"One of them," I forced out. My eyes flicked left to right, feeling as if everyone was looking at me. The picture was innocent. It could have been worse. But I still felt the violation of my privacy. We were just at a store. Why would someone take a secret photo of us and then post it on the Internet? We hadn't even started dating, and I didn't want even *this* amount of attention.

"You bought her a chessboard? Does she play?"

"I don't... I don't know. It's funny," I argued. "The pawns are elves and they're all smiling. It's like they're happy to go die for Santa and Mrs. Claus."

My parents and the high schoolers considered me with disturbed looks.

Swallowing, I swiped a hand over my bun. "Rose will think it's funny."

"I'm sure she will," Mom replied after a beat. But she didn't sound convinced. I didn't really care. I needed a quiet spot to think and regain my composure.

It's not a big deal. It's just a stupid picture.

But it was more than that. It was a microscope I didn't want to be under. A magnifying glass that would leave me burnt.

Twenty-Three

Will

THREE NIGHTS BEFORE CHRISTMAS

"We should tell your parents tonight," I said to Rose's profile. She was staring at something just past my shoulder, not registering I was even speaking. I followed her gaze.

Lawrence stood with his back to us.

"Rose." This time, I spoke with enough force in my voice to get her attention. "We need to end the lie. It's gone too far. I want to tell your parents tonight."

A crease formed between her eyebrows. "That we broke up or...?"

I shook my head, looking far more confident than I felt. "That we've been lying to them."

"No. Nope. They'll freak out."

"We are not pulling this off. We're going to get caught if we keep this up. It's better to get ahead of it."

"We're doing fine."

"I'm not keeping my distance from Lizzy, and I don't want to." I admitted with a heavy omission of fucking around in the basement. "And you"—I jerked my head in Lawrence's direction, where Rose's attention had already wandered—"are not being as discrete as you think, either."

She pinched the bridge of her nose.

"I don't want to keep lying. Particularly, not about Lizzy—"

"We are not telling my parents in the same conversation that we lied about dating *and* you having the hots for my sister," Rose interrupted.

Exhaling a deep breath, I agreed, "That's probably smart."

She smirked. "So, it's unlike us?"

"Practically opposites." I nudged her shoulder with mine. "We can wait a couple of days and announce an amicable breakup online."

"I really don't want to tell my mom and dad." She pleaded.

"I think we should." I scraped my toe on a black scuff mark on the tile floor. "We shouldn't have lied to them to begin with."

"Fine...we'll tell them tonight when we get home."

"Thanks."

I found Lizzy standing with her parents and a group of high schoolers. One of the orchestra kids held her phone in front of Lizzy's face. She stilled like she did when she was nervous.

I rubbed at the back of my neck, my muscles knotting into one. My throat closed, dreading what could be on that screen. With numb fingers, I slid my phone from my pocket and pulled up the show's most popular profile. The half a second it took for it to load was the longest in my life. My heart beat a panicked rhythm in my ears.

My breath rushed from my lungs. Relief washing over me and drying the cold sweat that had beaded on my forehead.

There was a picture of me and Lizzy, but it was as innocent as I could hope for. In the shot we were standing far enough apart, our facial expressions innocent. Some comments were suspicious, but nothing too bad. She had been nervous a few seconds ago, but she was probably experiencing the same wash of comfort I was.

If I needed any more reason to end the lie, dodging this bullet would have been it.

I turned to show Rose, only to find the space where she'd been at my side was empty and I hadn't even heard her leave. I'd been too absorbed in Lizzy.

I didn't bother to look if Lawrence were still with the group he'd been in.

I knew he wasn't.

My stomach dropped for the second time in less than a minute.

"Where's Rosie?" Kelly asked at my side. I jumped, caught off-guard yet again. The women of this family moved with incredible stealth.

Jim and Lizzy joined us.

I shoved my phone back into my pocket. My attempt to not look at Lizzy failed, instead I answered her mom while looking directly into Lizzy's eyes. "I don't know. She was just right here."

"We were just going to head out," Kelly explained. "She couldn't have gone far."

We'd all arrived together, piled in the family minivan. So, if Kelly said it was time to go, then it was time.

"I'll text her," I said, but Kelly was already walking down the hall toward the dark auditorium. Her heels clicking in contrast to the heavy footfalls of Jim's boots at her side, her arm hooked in his.

Lizzy chewed at the cuticles of her thumb, and I paused in typing the message to Rose. "What's wrong?"

Crossing her arms on her chest, Lizzy shook her head. "Nothing."

"Are you sure?"

The jerk of her head was the only answer she gave me. Turning, she followed her parents. Her back was ramrod straight.

Unease fitted back into my shoulders. I wanted to rush to her side, ask her if this was about the photo, but there were too many eyes around us.

I wasn't sure she wanted me near her, or worse, that she might actually *want* distance. Which was the exact opposite of what I wanted.

We'd had a fun day, been freer with each other than we should have been. But in the end, what I was offering her was empty. I was still hiding. The pale shadow of what we could become was bullshit if all I could give her was kisses in the dark and nothing else.

A loud gasp snapped my head up.

"Mom," Rose's surprised voice called from inside the opened door of the auditorium.

"What the hell?" Jim demanded louder than I'd ever heard him be before.

"Shit," a man hissed. I didn't have to see him to know, without a doubt, it was Lawrence.

My jaw tightened grinding my teeth. I took the last few steps through the open doors. The aisle lights in the floor were the only illumination in the spacious room. The darkness ate it up, leaving just the outlines of Lizzy and her family and Lawrence visible. The outline of a jaw, a shoulder, the angry wrinkles on Jim's forehead. Rose and Lawrence tucked into a darkened corner, standing far too closely as if they'd just been in each other's arms.

I knew this lie would blow up in our faces, but I thought it would be my fault.

It might have been naïve, but instead of anger or irritation, I felt sympathy for my friend who could have everything she wanted if she'd just let down her guard for a moment.

"I can explain," Rose tried.

"Explanation is unnecessary." Kelly shot a glance at me.

"Mom. Dad." Rose held her hands out, a silent plea in her palms.

Lawrence considered me out of the corner of his eye, as if guilt kept him from looking at me straight on. His weight was on the leg furthest from me, ready for an attack.

Jim placed a hand on my shoulder. "Don't do it. Not here."

I loosened the clench of my jaw, realizing how tightly bound my muscles were. It took a few seconds of focus to relax my stance. My concern must have looked like aggression with my hands fisted at my sides. No wonder Lawrence was watching me like I was a danger to him.

"It's time to go." Jim urged me to turn away, but my feet were still planted.

Unshed tears glistened in Rose's eyes. Lawrence's head hung in shame.

Just inside the door, Lizzy stood holding her elbow with one hand and the other pressed to her mouth. I wanted nothing more than to get her and her sister home. To take this mess we'd made somewhere private.

Scraping my palm over my lips, I nodded to Jim.

"Good for you, son," he spoke to my back.

It was my turn to hang my head.

Twenty-Four

Will

THREE NIGHTS BEFORE CHRISTMAS

The cold interior of the garage was almost a relief to the stifling tension of the van ride home. The only words spoken for the fifteen-minute drive were from Rose as soon as the last door had shut behind her dad. Three whispered syllables swallowed whole as soon as they were uttered, "I'm sorry."

She'd folded in on herself, startling when Lizzy reached across the space between their seats to give her wrist a reassuring squeeze.

Affection too big to be anything but love swelled in my chest. She was steadfast and tender. I was desperate to do right by her. After my short-lived marriage, I knew what it was to be in a toxic situation. I refused to put Lizzy through that, through *this*, any longer.

Jim hung his keys on the hook at the kitchen door, holding it open for his wife and daughters, and then me.

After depositing our boots on the mat by the door, the five of us paused in the kitchen. Lizzy at her sister's side, me on the other. Their parents had a silent conversation the way two people who knew and understood each other could.

Their family tension was painfully uncomfortable, squeezing at my insides. I could identify the illness, but I didn't have the immunities for it. My peacekeeping efforts wouldn't work here, it wasn't mine to keep.

With clear apprehension, Rose cast her eyes my way. I nodded back, knowing the silent question she asked.

Jim heaved a sigh, but Rose cut him off, her voice reed thin. "I have something to say. It'll make things clearer, but it won't make you think any better of me."

I wrapped my arm around her shoulders, squeezing her to my side. "Do you want me to say it?"

She shook her head. Wiping her nose on the sleeve of her blazer, she went on, "Bill and I date other people."

Kelly rolled her eyes—the gesture was exactly like her daughters.

"What is this hippy-dippy horseshit?" Jim growled. He pointed a finger at me. "So, you're okay with this, son?"

"We're just friends," Rose tried to explain.

"You and Lawrence?" Kelly demanded.

"No, me and Bill."

But Kelly continued talking as if Rose hadn't spoken. "That boy has been in love with you his entire life. Be with him or leave him alone."

"I tried," Rose said. Tears clung to her eyelashes.

"I want to stay out of your business." Kelly pressed her fingers to her forehead. "But then we catch you with your ex-boyfriend in the high school auditorium. *Half* the town was there! You're lucky it was us who found you."

"Or what, Mom?" Lizzy spoke up. "She'd ruin her reputation?"

"Lisianthus Marie." Kelly held up a finger in warning.

"Why are you so mad?" Gesturing a hand at me, still hugging Rose to my side, her shoulders rising and falling with shaky breaths. "Will isn't mad. Look at him. She's trying to talk to you. She's trying to be honest, and you won't listen. Sometimes you make it so hard. Just close your mouth and listen."

For a few moments, the only sounds were Rose's sniffles. She opened her mouth, but then she shut it again. After one more deep breath, she forced out, "Will and I aren't dating. We're just good friends. I lied to you—"

"We lied to you," I confirmed, shame burning my cheeks.

Kelly gripped the fabric of her blouse over her heart. Behind her, Jim took a step back. I had never felt so small.

Lizzy straightened her back. "Me too. I knew too."

Rose let out a watery chuckle that fortified her. "We thought it would help the show. And I needed an excuse to stay away from Lawrence, and you see how well that worked." Her words grew harsh. "Because I *know*, Mom."

Kelly blinked at the abrupt switch in Rose's tone.

She went on, "The audacity that you would know him more than me. *'His entire life,'* you don't say."

"Bring it back to the apology," Lizzy suggested, as I muttered, "Sounding less like sorry."

"Right."

"You lied about dating?" Deep furrows lined Jim's forehead.

"Isn't this just something famous people do?" Kelly asked.

"And people *trying* to be famous, apparently," I grumbled. The idea of telling her parents had been embarrassing, doing it was mortifying.

Rose swiped the heel of her hand across her wet cheeks. "Right, I am sorry."

"Me too." I wished I had a hole to crawl into. "We had it all reasoned out. It wasn't supposed to hurt you."

I resisted the urge to pace, choosing between what would be the right thing to do and how badly I didn't want to do it. Looking over Rose's head, I tried to burn into my memory the shape of Lizzy's lips, and the slope of her neck under the bun of her hair.

You'll see her again. But with the tension in the room too thick to take a normal breath, I couldn't ignore that I might have to fight for the chance.

Steeling myself, I breathed in a deep breath. "I'll find a ticket back to Kansas City."

Jim took in Rose, Lizzy, and then me. I held his eye, unwilling to show any cowardice—I wouldn't add that to the reasons he should hate me.

"To spend Christmas alone?" He crossed his arms over his chest.

"I'll be fine."

"No."

Kelly shot him a questioning look.

"That ice storm is rolling in, anyway. They'll be cancelling flights," he said to her, then he nodded once, as if decided. "You did a dumb thing. I don't know exactly what to think right now, but you're probably not a bad person. You might even be a good friend to my daughter—regardless of how hair-brained this whole idea was. You're staying. You're not spending Christmas alone."

I rubbed at the back of my neck. It was generous, more kind than I deserved. I didn't want to leave Rose to deal with the chaos I'd helped create.

Kelly sighed. "He's right, stay."

My gaze flicked to Lizzy, but she looked away as soon as our eyes met. It could be nothing. I could be paranoid reading her cues incorrectly, but my heart skittered.

With a completely unexpected change of subject, Kelly asked. "Who wants a snack?" She turned for the fridge. Then spoke with her face in the open door. "I'm too tuckered out for dinner. I've got half a cheeseball left over from the office party. Lizzy, will you grab the cookies out of the cupboard? Jim, will you get everyone a drink?"

Rose tilted her head, blinking. "Are we just done talking?"

Her mom shrugged, placing a tray on the counter. "I don't know what else to say. This is a lot to think about. But for the first time in so. Many. Years, I have two daughters that like being in the same room. And that makes me want to celebrate Christmas."

In a matter of minutes, we huddled around the counter with cheese, crackers, and cookies. I accepted the beer Jim offered. Anxiety slowly dissipated, releasing the tension in my shoulders. It wasn't gone, but it was better.

Eventually, Rose spoke up, "Can we talk about how sad the orchestra's *I'll be Home for Christmas* was?"

Lizzy nodded, her eyebrows shooting up. My fingers tingled to wipe away the red icing on the corner of her mouth. Not that I would under the circumstances. Not that it seemed like she'd want that right now.

"I thought it was boring," Jim said.

Kelly accepted the cracker spread with cheese her husband offered. "I didn't know that song could be ten minutes long."

Little by little, they fell into their normal pattern, chatting and playfully picking on each other. I smiled, but I was eager for an opportunity to talk to Lizzy alone. Something had upset her at the school before everything else happened. I wanted to know that she was all right. That we were all right.

After a few minutes, her parents went to the basement to watch *Prancer*, again. And Rose announced she was going to take a shower.

Lizzy wouldn't look at me, her head tipped down. I swallowed, my mouth suddenly dry.

Waiting, I let the silence stretch on until I couldn't take it any longer. Until my stomach had turned over too many times and I didn't feel well.

I leaned my elbows on the countertop. "You, okay?"

She shrugged. "Fine."

"You seem like you're not."

She jerked her shoulder again. Brushing the curls around her temple back, she took a drink of her wine.

"Was it just the stress of...everything?" I let the one word describe the Rose and Lawrence situation, and the following conversation with her parents.

She shook her head. She finally looked at me.

My pulse was heavy and sluggish. I saw what was coming while wishing to be wrong, hoping that I could say the right thing. Something that would set her at ease.

She set her glass down with a clink. "Did you see that picture of us?"

"Yeah, but it's not bad. The response seems...kind."

"Does that sort of thing happen often?"

"People recognizing me?"

"Sure, or strangers taking pictures of you and posting them online?"

My stomach churned. "Not often."

She'd gone perfectly still, and I understood the tell for what it was.

"Are you okay? Do you feel unsafe?" I asked.

"No. Nervous would be a better word."

"Why?"

"I just..." she swallowed. "I don't like it. I know it must seem small to you. But my social media is a LinkedIn for my work. I don't...I don't cultivate attention. I don't want it."

"We can keep our relationship quiet, private, just like you said we should. We could be more careful about how we are in public. Rose and I talked earlier about announcing a quote-en-quote breakup sooner rather than later. Lizzy, it doesn't happen often, I promise. You'll see that."

"Unless the show gets picked up."

"Even if that happens, we won't be famous. We'll have a slightly larger group of people who know us, but not a lot."

"I don't know..."

"I'll shield you from it."

"How?" The word was hardly more than air, as if her throat had grown tight.

I clenched my teeth, at a loss.

"It's okay," she sounded like she was trying to convince herself as much as me. "It was exciting while it lasted."

"No, don't talk like that. You know what happens less than a random posting a picture of me?" I waved my hand in the chasm growing between us. But she'd hidden her face. "*This*. A connection like this. I was drawn to you from the first time I saw you. And it's grown stronger every time since—every time I've kissed you, touched you. This is exceptional. I've never felt it before, and I'll never feel it again."

"How do you know?" she whispered.

It was so obvious. I couldn't believe that I had to say it aloud. "Because there is no other you."

She met my eyes, unshed tears clinging to hers. "I don't know if I can, Will."

"No, Lizzy," I pleaded.

"It's better to stop now. It'll just be harder later."

"It won't. It's already too hard. Come on. This isn't what either of us *wants*."

"Wanting something doesn't make it meant to be."

Reaching a hand to her face, I cupped her chin, urging her to meet my gaze. "But we are."

She shook her head and took a step back. It was the wrong direction. All of this was the wrong direction.

Two words laid my once flying hopes to rest. Buried. Dead.

"I can't."

Twenty-Five

Lizzy

SIX NIGHTS BEFORE CHRISTMAS

I stretched, sore in the best way, an echoing ache of the night before. My body remembering before my brain found consciousness. A big hand snaked up my hip, wrapping a powerful arm around my waist and pulling me against his chest. Will nuzzled his nose into my hair and groaned, rumbling against my back, quaking through my core, thundering in my chest. Such a small noise, for its overwhelming effect.

This was a morning I wanted to repeat over and over and over.

A lifetime of these mornings, I didn't know the silent prayer was in my mind until it was fully formed flying on wishful thinking.

"I could get used to this." Will's sleep worn voice in my ear.

"Yeah," I answered lamely, suddenly conscious of how bad my breath must be.

Moving my hair from my naked shoulder, his lips drew a random constellation on my skin. My self-consciousness disappeared with every burst of sensation until a sigh escaped my lips and I was languid under his attention. He urged me onto my back, his elbows on either side of my face supporting his weight. My eyelids fluttered open. Above me, he took me in.

"I didn't expect you, Lizzy."

Something that had laid dormant possibly my entire life, stirred in my chest. A reckless desire that I gave myself too freely. With only a single night of proof. A few hours of connection. A deep, unexplained *knowing*. I gave myself to something more substantial than hope.

This beautiful man was mine.

And I was wasted to all other men in his wake.

The scruff on his cheek and jaw scraped against my palm. His expressive eyes rolled and closed, overwhelmed by my touch.

"I've never liked the unexpected before," I said. "But I like this."

Lowering, he pressed a tender kiss to my mouth. My leg hooked over his hip—twining us together in the most natural way.

The morning just kept getting better and better.

Twenty-Six

Will

TWO NIGHTS BEFORE CHRISTMAS

The storm had grounded all flights coming and going from west and central Michigan. It was just a matter of time before the weather hit Flint and Detroit, shutting down their airports. So, even if I wanted to take the risk of the drive across the state, I'd just be trapped there instead of here.

Which I was still considering.

The only reason I was lying on my back in the spare bedroom while feeling sorry for myself. Instead of driving through the ice storm while feeling sorry for myself, was because ice storms were dangerous, and the rental car had barely adequate tires. Ice pinged against the windowpane above my head. Irritatingly enough, it reminded me of the first night I'd met Lizzy.

The sudden dark of the bar, my hand on her waist to balance her. My first glimpse of her dimples when she smiled. Her slow thawing was like a reward forgetting to know her.

How had we met only a few days ago? How was I in such a sad state after only a handful of moments?

Because being with her feels like electricity.

I groaned and scraped a hand across my face. I wished, again, for something to do. A task to keep my hands busy. A nail to hammer. Something to turn my brain quiet. The familiar satisfaction of creating something—of a job done.

Then, as if conjured, the high-pitched buzz of a power tool brought me sitting straight on the bed. My feet were on the carpet and moving toward the closed door before I realized what I was doing. Stepping into the hallway, a mixture of hope and anxiety surged through me at the possibility of finding myself face-to-face with Lizzy.

Her door was closed.

Rose and Kelly were in the kitchen wearing flour covered aprons. The oven heated the room. The scent of their cookies baking was a manifestation of Christmas.

Except for Lizzy missing from this adorable tableau.

I hated to think that it might be my fault that she wasn't spending time with her family. It twisted my gut to imagine her in her bedroom feeling as terrible as I did. My only recourse was to leave her alone.

The corners of Kelly's lips turned down, and she nodded at her daughter with appreciation. "Goodness, you called that."

I lifted an eyebrow at Rose.

She shrugged. "I told Mom the drill would get you out of the room."

"And then you were here." Kelly gestured toward me with two giant oven mitts covering her hands. "Jim's in the garage."

I hadn't seen much of him since the conversation from the day before. It was possible my existence still irritated him. It was for sure that I was uncomfortable around him...but the *power tools.*

I shoved my fists in my pockets. "Do you think he'd mind if I helped?"

"He'll appreciate the help," Kelly answered with confidence.

I didn't believe her, but the prospect of doing something was too great to turn down. The whiz of the drill started again, and I followed it like a siren's call.

The minivan was parked in one of the garage stalls, the other acted as a woodworking shop. He hunched over a board suspended on work horses. To his credit, instead of rolling his eyes when he saw me, he jerked his chin in welcome. I closed the kitchen door behind me. The scent of wood shavings and motor oil were even more comforting than the cookies. I swung my arms, my hands hitting my thighs with a smack, unsure of what body language would be correct in this instance. At least his attention had returned to the two planks of wood he was screwing together.

"What do ya got goin' here?" I asked.

"A bookshelf for a friend's grandkid."

"Nice..." I nodded, more bobble head like than human. "Can I help?"

He grunted in what seemed like affirmation.

Though he had it in hand on his own, I folded myself into his task. For a few minutes we didn't speak—just passed tools back and forth. When we started adding the shelves, he asked, "You've never dated my daughter?"

My shoulders fell. The silence had been too good to last. "No, Rose and I have always just been good friends."

"Why? Don't you think she's beautiful?"

"Of course she is." My tongue grew a few sizes too large in my mouth, and I struggled not to jumble my words together. "It's just never been there."

"What hasn't?"

"Attraction, I guess."

He made a *huh* sound in the back of this throat. Speaking with his eyes on his work, he started, "I'm gonna ask a blunt question."

Trepidation tangled my stomach in knots. "Okay…"

"What are your feelings for Lizzy?"

Oh shit.

I leaned a hip against the workbench. Crossing my arms, I searched for the best way to explain. How much should I say? *What* should I say? He waited in patient silence.

"We met the night before I got here." I searched every corner of my brain for the words to explain to him while also keeping my foot securely out of my mouth. "I like her a lot. More than I've liked anyone in a long time."

He paused in his task, his brow furrowed.

"I thought…we could…" I tried to continue, but my convoluted thoughts were unintelligible and half-formed explanations. "Date."

It was such an inadequate word for what I thought Lizzy and I could be. What else was I supposed to say to her dad?

Well, Jim, after just a few days of knowing your daughter, Lizzy, I want to devote the rest of them to her. But she doesn't want the same.

"Anyway, last night she told me she's not interested in a relationship because of how public my life is."

His jaw set, and a line formed between his thick pale eyebrows.

I scraped my palm along my jaw. "I don't even blame her. It's gotten kinda crazy." Heat warmed my cheeks. "I've…It's as if, in chasing a modicum of fame and fortune, I've lost some sense of myself. Lately, my choices have been embarrassing at best. I am not exactly inspiring confidence at the moment."

"Would you give up the show for her?"

"Honestly, I'm questioning if I want it."

Jim fixed me with a glare. "You better figure out what you want or you're going to break both of my girls' hearts. Rose wants this show, and Lizzy clearly sees something in you."

The urge to ask him what he meant by that was hard to ignore, but he didn't seem like he'd be willing to explain. And asking would make me look desperate—which I was. But hopefully, he didn't know that.

"I understand," I said.

He grunted, setting back to the task at hand. "Sounds like you got a lot to think about."

I did.

We went back to assembling the bookshelf while not speaking. The quiet was a relief with my thoughts were so loud.

Twenty-Seven

Lizzy

TWO NIGHTS BEFORE CHRISTMAS

"The coast is clear. Open your door," Rose said instead of knocking.

I leaned forward to set my laptop on my bedside table, my muscles and joints stiff from sitting with terrible posture against my headboard. With awkward rigid steps, I crossed my room.

She held a plate on the other side of the door piled high with chocolate chip and snickerdoodle cookies. For hours, enticing smells had seeped into my room, just like it did every year. I'd considered going into the garage to help Dad, but then I heard Will heading that way.

Instead, I watched Christmas specials of my favorite TV shows and texted Shay. She relayed that Lawrence was more withdrawn than usual. I'd had to tell her what had happened the day before. Rose was lucky there was a storm keeping Shay at her parents. But she wasn't holding back her angry texts. I didn't stop her. She was protective.

With Rose and Lawrence's past, she had reason to be.

God only knew the hell Shay was giving him.

Rose and I were healing our relationship. But it was still clear she didn't know what she was doing. I didn't understand why she wouldn't be with him. They seemed like they were still in love.

But then, I could see myself loving Will and I'd taken a step back.

Doing scary things was hard.

"Cookie?" She held the plate directly under my nose. As if I could have said no.

I peeked down the hall around her shoulder. "How do you feel about grabbing a glass of milk?"

"Thermos under my arm."

I moved to make room for her to enter. "Thank you."

"You're welcome." Her eyes swept over the periwinkle walls and bedroom furniture I'd chosen in high school. Including my desk with my color coded sticky notes and pens. "So, your taste is the same."

I rolled my eyes. "I'm here temporarily."

"I guess I could have a time capsule room if I'd stayed closer to home too."

"Would you want one?" The cookie was still warm when I picked it up off the plate. The chocolate dripped in my mouth.

"No."

"Me either."

She snorted. "Then why are you here?"

"Do you know these people don't charge rent? They make me call them Mom and Dad, but free-living, are you kidding me?"

It was so good to make her laugh. It had been a weird week of emotional ups and downs. But in all of that, *this* had happened. My heart was more broken than it should have been. Yet my sister was bringing me cookies and laughing at my jokes. Ups and downs.

"That sounds pretty good." She picked up a snickerdoodle and held out her hand for me to pass the thermos of milk. "How long do you think you'll live here?"

"I'm not sure. My business is doing okay, actually."

"That's outstanding!" She beamed at me with crumbs at the corners of her mouth. "I was so impressed when I heard you were doing this. It takes guts."

"It was a big change."

"I wasn't disappointed to hear your ex wouldn't be around."

"I always wondered if you hated him."

"Kinda. He just never seemed to realize how cool you are."

"You think I'm cool?"

"The coolest." She nodded to the floor. Neither of us could look at one another with so much subtext. I was about to change the subject when she blurted, "I'm sorry."

My jaw slackened. "What?"

"For...the past eight years—"

"That wasn't just you," I said, but she kept going.

"—for not telling you I was thinking of schools out of state. For making you out to be a...loser." She turned her head, looking right into my eyes. "You're not. I was so angry and jealous of anyone who got to hang out with you. And I took it out on you. I'm really sorry."

The tender wounds of my heart were a little less painful under the salve of her words. "I'm sorry too. I wish I had been less selfish and more understanding. I get it now, how you needed to grow without me."

She made a *hmm* sound. "I don't want to grow alone anymore."

It felt corny to wrap my arms around her shoulders. To lean into her hug for the healing nature of it. I gave her support just as much as I received hers.

Pulling away, we both wiped fingertips under our eyes and laughed.

I jerked my head toward my laptop. "I was just about to watch the New Girl episode where they yell at the rich neighborhood and Nick misses his flight."

"Turn on the lights!" she quoted.

"Yes, exactly!"

She scooted back on the bed in a similar position I'd just been in, leaving room for me to sit next to her. "Can we watch the one with all the Christmas parties after?"

"The one where Winston *might* still believe in Santa?"

"Yes!"

We were halfway through the first episode—the plate of cookies devoured—when Dad and Will's voice carried from the kitchen to my room. I couldn't make out what they were talking about, but just the sound of Will's voice was enough to make my chest ache and my blood to heat.

"You, okay?" Rose asked.

I nodded, even though I didn't feel okay.

She paused the show. "You wanna tell me your side?"

I made a disgusted sound. Setting my laptop on the mattress by our feet, I shifted to face her. "So, Will and I had discussed dating privately when you two are done with...you know."

She rolled her eyes and nodded.

"I thought I could get past, like, how public your lives are. Or I just kinda assumed I wouldn't be interesting. But that photo of us shopping..."

"Gotcha. I can see how that violates your privacy. You don't even have an Insta, do you? I can never find you when I look."

"You look for me?"

"Of course. I mean, Mom and Dad give me updates, but they only know what parents know. They don't know you like Shay does. They don't know you the way I *want* to know you. So, I look for you sometimes just to get a different glimpse of your life."

A sad smile tilted my lips. "I had to force myself to stop checking your profiles. It wasn't easy."

"I get it."

"Anyway, that photo freaked me out. You know what I'm like. I hate attention, especially from strangers. I was all wrapped up in weird anxiety and then I told him I wasn't even willing to try a relationship. Which sucks even more because he's here for the next week and a half."

"He looked for flights, but the storm."

I flinched. A dull ache started at the base of my skull. "He's leaving?"

"He was thinking about it. Would you be disappointed if he did?"

"Probably."

She looked at me out of the corner of her eye, one eyebrow raised.

"Yeah," I admitted, "I would."

"Do you wanna talk to him?"

"I don't know if I should." If only the answer could be the simple *yes*, I wanted it to be, but it wasn't. "I was so uncomfortable, and I just wanted to hide."

She chewed on her lower lip. "It just sucks, because it doesn't happen often. But one time was enough for you, I get that. It just amps up when things happen. We announced our relationship, so there are more eyes on us. When we breakup, it's going to happen. If you two announce you're dating—"

"If you get the show," I interjected.

"*If* we get the show," she conceded. "That's a big *if*. You're still my sister. It might happen when you're with me."

"That's a good point." The prospect of the two of us just hanging out filled me with so much joy.

"Speaking of..." She crossed her legs to her side, angling herself in my direction. "I have something I want you to think about."

"Okay..."

Her words fell out as if they were running downhill. "I have a spare room, and I want you to move into it."

"You do?" My grin was so big.

"I've really liked this. I don't want to pause reconnecting. You said living here was temporary, anyway. If you just pay for your own food, and your expenses. I'll cover everything else. You won't even have to call me Mom and Dad."

I snorted. It was surreal. A week ago, I would have felt grateful just to have her acknowledge my existence. I could never have expected this. "Okay, I'll move in with you."

Her smile was all teeth. It reminded me of our childhood Christmas mornings. "You don't want to think about it or anything?"

"No."

"Well, good."

"Good." I pictured what living with her would be like—spending time together, learning about each other again, fighting like sisters. I felt good. Right.

Even if I might be included in the friendly fire of fan's photos. I wouldn't trade the chance to have her in my life for that.

A thought took shape, startling in its clarity. Fear gripped my sternum. I wanted to hide from it. But I wouldn't.

Rose considered me out of the corner of her eye. "You look glum. Did you change your mind already?"

"No," I grumbled, then rolled my eyes.

"I have an idea," I heaved a heavy sigh. "And I hate it."

Twenty-Eight

Will

ONE NIGHT BEFORE CHRISTMAS

I ignored my phone buzzing in my pocket. Jim stapled a piece of trim into place as I held it along the ceiling.

When a family party was canceled because of the treacherous roads, I'd wondered how I would withstand another day in this house. The roads were also why I was still Kelly and Jim's guest. I was stuck right where I was.

Early in the morning, I'd gone into the kitchen in search of coffee. To find Jim drinking from a mug. "Wanna help me with my 'Honey-do' list? A couple of things would be easier with two people. Lizzy would help, but she's been busy with work. Anyway, you in?"

I was. I *really* was.

Holding still was challenging for me under normal circumstances. Holding still while snowed in with a woman I couldn't stop thinking about—a woman who had already turned me down...

I was desperate for distraction.

Kelly was ecstatic to find us working through the list.

It was mid-morning, but we'd already crossed a few things off the list. We should move slower. I dreaded finding the end of the work.

My phone buzzed insistently as we took a step back, inspecting the trim now secure to the wall. Finally, the vibrating stopped only to start back up.

"Looks good," Jim jerked his head in approval.

I'd done a hell of a lot harder carpentry than this. Which made it laughable how much his approval meant. He'd painted the black crown molding to match the black built in shelving. It was an intense look. But the more I'd gotten to know Kelly, the more it fit.

"You gonna answer that?" he asked, my phone starting up again.

"Seems like maybe I should." I pulled my phone from my pocket to find Rose on the caller ID. Pressing it to my ear, I asked, "Aren't you in the other room?"

"*Finally,*" she groaned.

"What's up?"

"Check the Live that just posted."

"On our page?"

She made a disgusted sound. "Yes."

Foregoing the social structures of a 'goodbye', she disconnected the call. My lips pressed into a thin line. I searched for patience to deal with her bossing me around—all the time. In her defense, I was usually fine with it. I was slightly more irritable than usual.

"Uh, if you'll give me just a second," I said to Jim, taking a step toward the spare room. He grunted his agreement.

I opened the app to find the most recent post featured Lizzy and Rose sitting side-by-side wearing Christmas sweaters. Rose beamed at the camera, but Lizzy was giving it a side-eye that I felt in my chest.

She'd signed her name on my heart with those knives for eyes. Even if it'd been a brief time, her effect would last.

I moved down the hall to find privacy in the spare room. With the door closed behind me, I breathed out a calming breath. My thumb hovered over the reel. Tilting my head, a crease pressed between my eyebrows. I tapped on the post. Through my speaker, *Rose spoke to Lizzy, "Can you pretend to be happy to be here?"*

Scoffing, she replied, "No."

Rose laughed, rolling her eyes. "Fine. Hello everyone, I hope you're enjoying your holidays! It's been a really interesting time...here."

"Interesting," Lizzy agreed.

"Anyway, I don't know how much I've mentioned my twin sister, Anne, or I guess sometimes you go by Lizzy."

Looking square in the camera, she said, "Like, all the time."

With a smirk, Rose shook her head. "Fine. I'm the only one that wants to call you Anne. The point of all of this is that she will be around more. She is moving in with me, and you might catch glimpses of her—like a beloved house cat skittering out of the shot."

My heart swelled too big for my ribs. It was such a different message than that metaphor had served earlier this week. Instead of derision, she used it with affection. They would be okay and could continue repairing the damage done to their relationship. If I couldn't be with Lizzy, at least she and Rose could have each other.

Lizzy would continue to be in my orbit. I'd just have to ignore her gravity. Just like the moon could ignore the pull of earth.

I resented the jealousy I felt taking away from the appreciation I had for Lizzy and Rose's healing relationship, but I couldn't help the knowing that Lizzy would tolerate some attention for Rose, but not for me. Even if it was fair that their relationship was more meaningful than hers and mine.

"This concession, if you can't tell by how she is glaring at the camera," *Rose went on, "is truly an act of love on her part. So, we wanted to introduce her to you. But we have a greater purpose for showing up on your feeds."*

She turned her head, giving the camera her profile and directing the attention to Lizzy. Her cheeks were bright pink, and she'd gone still.

I knew they'd already filmed and posted, but I still felt the urge to tell Rose to back off. To put my body between Lizzy and the people watching on the livestream. Their reactions floating up the side of the screen like silent announcements that all eyes were on her.

Taking her hand, Rose squeezed it.

Lizzy kept her eyes down on her lap. Her voice was almost too quiet for the microphone to pick up, as she said, "I take it back."

Blind, stupid hope surged through me. There was no knowing what "it" was, but I wanted that sentence to be for me. I begged for it in the whispering corners of my heart to be for me.

"I hope you'll let me take it back." Lizzy's softened gaze met the camera. "I want to try."

A flurry of hearts fluttered up the screen—like butterflies taking flight.

Rose grinned at her sister with tender pride. "Good job," she mouthed.

"Thanks," Lizzy mouthed back.

"That's it from us. Anne and I hope you're having happy holidays, too."

The video stopped, frozen, with Lizzy focused on the camera through her eyelashes. My pulse thundered in my ears.

'I want to try.'

'Us' equaled her and me.

I'd spent the last two days fighting, and losing, against my disappointment. Struggling to accept that the relationship I desperately wanted with her wasn't possible. And in just a few short sentences, she'd changed the trajectory. We weren't written in the stars just yet, but if she would try, then we *could* be.

I would. Happily.

Before exiting the room, I grabbed the only gift I hadn't already placed under the Christmas tree. The hallway was empty. It only took two footsteps to stand outside of Lizzy's bedroom door. But it took me two attempts at knocking before I was successful.

Sweat prickled at the back of my neck, waiting the few seconds for her to open the door. A hallow of moisture formed around my fingers on the shiny wrapping paper in my hands.

The latch clicked as she twisted the knob. She leaned a shoulder against the doorjamb, biting her lower lip. Still clad in the adorable, ridiculous Christmas sweater she'd worn in the video—a kitten lying on its back playing with a Christmas tree ornament. She rolled the fabric between her fingertips.

Hugging the present to my chest in a way that did not make me feel masculine, I pinched it under one arm instead. I stuffed my hands in the pockets of my jeans to keep from fidgeting with my hands. Or pulling her against me. She'd said we could try, but she hadn't said that we could with her parents just down the hall. She might still want to be private.

"Did you see it?" she asked.

A smile split across my face. "Yeah."

Her head remained pointed toward her slippers. "I'm so sorry to go back and forth like this. It's not fair, and if you've changed your mind."

The need to touch her grew too strong, even if she wanted to keep us a secret for a while longer. Hooking a knuckle under her chin, I eased her to meet my gaze. "I haven't."

Her brown eyes slipped over my face, taking in my smile and the happiness alight in my gaze. "You're still willing to try?"

"I'm desperate to."

The soft pressure of her touch sliding up my chest to my shoulders drew hot lines across my skin. Even through my clothes, my body remembered her touch as if she were tattooing me. Forever branded by her.

I cupped her face in one hand and pressed my palm to her back, my fingers splayed.

The gift smacked on the carpeted floor. At least it wasn't breakable. But it was distracting enough. She paused, looking at it laying between our feet.

"What's that?" she asked.

My voice caught in my throat, suddenly self-conscious that I'd brought it. "It's just a little gift. It's probably lame to give it to you now."

"I like it when you're lame." She beamed at me as she bent to pick it up. "Can I open it now?"

I shrugged. "Sure. Just don't make fun of me too badly."

"I don't make any promises." She pulled on the ribbon I'd tied around the package. The tape released with a pop, and in only a few seconds, the paper pealed away, revealing the planner's pink cover.

She blinked up at me.

My toes curled and uncurled on the carpet. "If you want to collect planners and never use them...you should collect planners and never use them."

Her lips pulled up at the corners, and I melted in her warmth. The space between our bodies closed in increments. Her mouth pulled mine to hers. Breath by breath. She possessed a magnetism I could surrender to.

"Thank you," she whispered, peppermint on her breath.

I pulled her against my chest. Where I knew she belonged. I'd known it since the moment I'd sat next to her in the hotel bar.

She fit. We fit.

Her mouth was warm and soft.

Finally, I could give her all of me. We didn't have to be secretive or hide.

At the end of the hall, Jim mumbled, "I told you so."

I could practically hear Kelly roll her eyes. "Yeah, yeah, you called it."

Lizzy pulled away, leaving me drunk on just her kiss. Tucking her head into my neck, she held me and let me hold her. It was a rare moment.

It was right.

Twenty-Nine

Lizzy

CHRISTMAS DAY

"It's freezing out there," Will hissed, slipping back under the covers of my bed.

His toes touched my calf, and I yipped. "Jesus! Did you go to the bathroom or the arctic?"

"Oo"—he wrapped powerful arms around my waist, pulling me back to his chest—"you're so warm."

Giggling, I squirmed. "I was. You're taking my heat."

He shifted his hips, nestling closer to my ass, his erection against the round curve of my cheek. Suddenly inspired, I shifted closer instead of further away. Gliding a hand down my thigh, he groaned. "The wiggling is nice."

"You're nice."

"Not as nice as you."

I burst out laughing. He shushed me, pressing his rough fingertips to my lips.

My shoulders shook, but I managed to stay quiet. I whispered, "You're so much nicer than me. Remember when you met me?"

His fingers traced the seam of my lips. Heat pooled in my core. A call and response.

He ran his hand down the column of my throat. He had to feel my blood rushing hot just under the tender skin. "I remember everything about meeting you."

"Then you should recall that I'm not very nice." My words were barely more than puffs of air.

"Clearly, we have two different versions of that night." Palming my ass, he squeezed. "Goddamn."

In the back of my throat, I moaned.

"Stay quiet. I want to stay here, and I definitely don't want to wake up your family. This is the best Christmas morning I've ever had."

"The absolute best?"

"Couldn't get better."

I ground my hips into his, thrilled at his sharp intake of breath. "Couldn't?"

"I don't think you can stay quiet enough."

"I can."

"What about the basement?"

"That was one time."

My body arched at the progress of his touch.

"Lizzy," he breathed my name in my ear, then pressed a kiss to my neck. "We have time. We'll have other mornings like this"—he pulled me tighter against him, his arms solid bans around my ribs—"just let me hold you."

I sighed. The heat and tension in my body were still there, but his words helped calm me. With the intimacy I found just being with him, I snuggled even closer.

"This is more than enough," he whispered

⁂

"Will had the idea of giving you my favorite things." I handed Rose the heavy overstuffed basket. Initially, I'd felt trepidation about the suggestion. That was gone now. I wanted her to know me. They were just *things*, but we'd shared so many before. The line between hers and mine were blurred when we were young. This gift was a little like that.

"So cute!" Mom beamed. She cuddled into my dad's side on the loveseat, his arm pulling her closer. Logs burned in the fireplace. It crackled and smelled like past Christmases trapped in the amber of my memory.

Mom, Rose, and I had fuzzy socks pulled up our calves. We'd discarded the blankets that had been on our laps. They lay in knitted puddles on the carpet. Dad kept eyeing the windows behind me and Will. He would open one any minute now.

But the fire would continue burning.

Just another Christmas tradition.

I sat crisscross applesauce next to Will, with the tree on my other side. He had one leg stretched out in front of him. His elbow propped on the knee of the other. Every once in a while, I'd glance in his direction to find him looking back with the most heartwarming affection.

I couldn't stop grinning.

We were one of those weird families that took turns opening presents.

All eyes were on Rose as she unfolded the chunky knit blanket off the top of the basket. I'd had to wash mine before giving it to her. There wasn't time to order a new one. It made me happy to give her mine. Being overly sentimental seemed to be the theme of the day.

She held it to her face. "My God, this is so soft."

"Isn't it lovely?"

"Hey," she exclaimed, setting the blanket aside and pulling two jars out, "I have these candles!"

"Do you really?!"

"Yes! They're my favorite too!"

We shared matching smiles, and Will rubbed a thumb up and down the back of my neck. My heart rate jumped, not just at his touch, but because it wasn't in secret. Once Will and I had made up yesterday, Rose posted about her and Will's breakup. She told their fans not to be sad, that they were both happier as friends. That their time trying out a romantic relationship had been the strangest few days of their lives. That it was a relief to be nothing more than pals again.

I hadn't ventured onto the Internet since then.

Rose's mouth pulled to one side, looking down at the basket's contents. "This is the weirdest chess set."

Mom lifted her eyebrows, her lips pursed.

"It's so funny," Rose continued.

I shot my mom an, *I told you so* face.

She rolled her eyes, but there was a pleased glint in them.

"Why are the elves so happy?" Holding the box, Rose showed the front image to everyone. "They're pawns. They're being used."

"That's what I said! And the gingerbread men bishops? That implies a strange religion."

"Mr. And Mrs. Clause hold an interesting court."

"I love the reindeer knights, though."

"They are cute."

"What was the other one?" Will leaned forward for a better look. The curve where his neck and shoulder connected became my sole focus until I remembered he'd asked a question.

"The rooks are snowmen." Rose and I said in unison.

"Gotcha." Settling back, he draped an arm around my waist.

She nodded. "Yeah, they're kinda a bummer."

"The elves are the big winners," I agreed.

"Clearly."

The combination of my relationship with Rose repairing, and the love blooming in my heart for Will, had me giddy with Christmas spirit. I was practically Buddy the Elf.

Stop being so corny.

But I couldn't help it. My sister and I were not only on speaking terms, but friends again. My parents were being incredibly cool about the turn of events.

And Will, with his sexy hands, was mine.

I was happy and grateful.

Being bold was really paying off.

Will's arms wrapped around my ribs. I breathed in the clean smell of his skin.

He kissed the top of my head. "God, I want time to stop."

Laying my head on his chest, I tried to nuzzle into him as much as I could. "Me too."

"Maybe I could push back my flight."

He and Rose were scheduled to fly home in four days.

"I won't be far behind you. I'm going to start packing within the minute you leave."

"Promise?"

"Promise."

I ignored the movie on the basement television screen, too busy absorbing every detail that I could of Will. It would only be a few weeks of missing him. I could make it.

Even if I didn't want to.

Deprivation had never concerned me much. It did this time.

There are phones and the Internet. It'll be fine.

He might have been thinking the same thing or sensed how my heart was growing heavy because his arms pulled me in even tighter.

Footsteps moved down the hall. Unlike our first time alone in the basement, we didn't have to pray that we wouldn't be caught.

The door to the garage opened, and the sound of large boots on the floor overhead was distinct and out of place—considering it was well after midnight. A man's voice drifted down the stairs. I recognized it was Lawrence, but he and Rose were too quiet to make out any of their words. They went back and forth, their tones changing from irritated to vulnerable.

"There's no logic in the way I feel about you." His voice had notched a little louder, anger biting at every word. When he continued, he was too quiet again.

But his pain echoed in my head.

They must have been standing so close. Close enough to hold each other. It lasted for minutes.

Why can't they just be together?

I'd asked myself this question so many times over the years. Every time, I recalled all the steps that had brought them down this path. Even just the few fights I'd seen were full of words sharp enough to cut. They were never careful enough. Never kind enough.

Eventually, he left. One step after another was all it took, but the weight of him lingered. Rose remained, glued to her spot for a few moments after the door closed, before retreating to her bedroom.

When it was clear she was gone, Will said, "That seemed...depressing."

"I don't ever want to hurt like that." I used to think that I didn't want love like that either, but I suspected it was too late for me now.

Will hooked a finger under my chin. His eyes held mine with a burning intensity. He was staring into the deepest parts of me and wasn't looking away.

"I just want to be good to you," he promised.

Thirty

Lizzy

AFTER CHRISTMAS

I'd be goddamned if Will didn't fill out a cable-knit sweater like a cozy Greek God. He was all sweet, yet masculine charm with a puppy sleeping in his palm, its head nuzzled on his shoulder. The humane society director, Patricia, had gotten the shots she wanted of Will and Rose. Then she left us to cuddle with the two puppies for as long as we wanted.

"Please, take your time," Patricia said as she waved goodbye. "They need the socialization."

"Well, if they need it," Rose joked.

At the door, Patricia paused. A rare hesitant expression fit onto her face. "It might not be my place to say, but I see how you two make better friends."

With a wink in my direction, she left, closing the door behind her.

Like always, my eyes found Will. He was their favorite thing. A crease pressed between his eyebrows. His lips tilted to one side.

"Did Patricia just give you two her blessing?" Rose asked.

I snorted. "I wasn't asking for it, but I'll take it."

"She's good people."

I nodded. My butt was going numb from sitting on the tile floor, but I also had a sleeping puppy on my lap, and I didn't want to disturb her. She was lying on her back in the valley between my thighs, her paws flopped at her chest. Her little belly rose and fell with even breaths.

"Most people are," Will added.

"Let's not be hasty," I said, as Rose stated, "I'm gonna stop you right there."

We broke into silent laughter. It came to an abrupt stop when the puppy on my lap groaned.

"Maybe we can adopt her." Rose brushed her fingertips on the soft triangle ear. "She could be our show dog. Maybe that would get our show on a streaming service."

She'd remained silent about the midnight visit from Lawrence. Occasionally, I'd catch her with a thousand-yard stare, as if she was considering removing one of her limbs. But she was still laboring under her thoughts alone.

"You think a dog is more enticing than the relationship roller coaster you've put your fans through?" I asked.

"Look at her."

She was a perfect little dog, a black lab mix with a wrinkled nose.

"You make a fine point," I conceded.

"Would you be really disappointed if we didn't get streaming?" Will gently unhooked a mini claw from his sweater.

Rose shrugged, but I suspected that she was faking her nonchalance. "I'd be disappointed. Not, like, crushed. You?"

His eyes shot to me, then to his toes.

Is he concerned about how it would affect me?

"Not crushed."

"I hope you two get it," I said.

"You do?" they asked at the same time.

For a moment, their shock made me feel guilty. Pushing it aside, I looked at them. "Of course I do. It still freaks me out to be...I don't know. Noticed. But I want you to have whatever you want. I'll be okay."

Rose leaned her head on my shoulder. "Thanks."

With the toe of his shoe, Will bopped my boot. He looked at me with his kind green eyes, and I felt like I was the cutest thing in the room.

I was already dreading tomorrow when they'd leave for Kansas City. They hadn't even left yet, but I could feel the hole they'd leave behind. Even if it'd only be for a few weeks.

Moving back home had been fine, in an embarrassing blow to my ego kind of way. I couldn't wait to move again. Rose sent me Pinterest boards of bedroom styles we could do to my new room. Every one of them featuring a desk as the focal point.

"Someplace to show off your stationary collection," she explained. "Why would it be so pretty if you're not going to show it off?"

Why, indeed.

Once, moving had signified the end of my old life. This time, it was a beginning. One where Rose and I could be sisters. One where Will and I could continue to grow this connection between us. Our strange beginning was turning out to be the perfect way for us to start. I had evidence of his kindness and consistency, the lengths he would go for someone he cared for. It made trusting him so easy.

Will and Rose waved over their shoulders as they went through security. Convincing my arms to let him go had been the most challenging thing. Somehow, I'd done it—committing the beat of his heart and his clean scent to something deeper than memory. He was still in eyesight, but I missed him desperately.

Mom hooked an arm around my shoulders. "You two are cute."

I rolled my eyes. "Thanks, Mom."

"Let's go home."

It might have been rude to walk through the airport with my eyes cast down toward my phone, but I pulled it from my pocket, anyway. With the notes app open, I started my packing list. A text came through, and a silly thrill shot through me.

Will: You packing yet?

I sent back a screen shot.

Me: I promised.

Thirty-One

Epilogue

LIZZY

Will held out his hand for my coat. He hung it on a hook at the front entrance of his second-floor apartment. His place fit him so well. Industrial beamed ceiling with gleaming woodwork throughout. The small space was thoughtfully utilized and cozy. He'd given me a tour of the wood shop on the main floor of his building. Downstairs, he'd seemed more comfortable than he was in his apartment.

His fingers twitched at his sides, and he licked his lips.

He gestured to the room. "This is my place."

"I like it," I said.

"It's not too..." Pink rose up his throat to his cheeks, and my heart ached.

"Too what?"

"I don't know." His biceps flexed distractingly as he rubbed at the back of his neck. After moving me into Rose's place the day before, he'd given me a kiss goodbye and not much more. And while we were on our 'first date' just a few moments ago, he'd behaved like a total gentleman. I had yet to jump his bones since arriving in Kansas City.

The rise and fall of his chest paired with the way his T-shirt matched the green of his eyes were almost too handsome to hear over. "Boring. Male. Small."

I scoffed. "You just helped me move from my parents' house into my sister's. No. I'm not judging the size or decor of the space that you own. I do really like it, though."

The heel of my boot clicked on the tile floor by the front door. It took no time at all to close the space between us. I leaned against him, my hands resting on his chest.

His hands slid from my hips to the back pockets of my jeans. "I really like you in it."

For our date, he'd taken me to a barbecue place, claiming that it would change my life. It was really good. But considering how my life was going...I'd already made the changes I was interested in. Now, I was looking forward to some consistency—with Will firmly established in my usual routine.

Going up on my tiptoes, I placed a kiss on his neck just below his jaw. His stubble was rough on my lips. "Wanna give me a tour of your bedroom?"

"You don't want a drink first?"

I fell back onto my heels. Pursing my lips, I didn't even pretend to appreciate his suggestion. "Will, it has been a month and a half."

A cocky grin spread across his face. It would have been annoying if I didn't like him so much. "You've been keeping track?"

"Haven't you?" I demanded. "A. Month. And. A. Half. Since we had to be quiet in the basement. I've been surviving"—I lifted a haughty eyebrow—"*admirably*, on sexting, and solicited dick pics. Do you want me to beg?"

His eyebrows shot up, and he tilted his head to the side.

My mouth fell open, the corners pulled up. I slapped his chest in the most girlish way. "You do, don't you?"

"You bring out the weirdest sides of me." He kissed me deep and slow. I unraveled. My tight coils puddled in a tangle that didn't feel messy. On the contrary, the more I revealed to him, the more certain I was that he appreciated all my sharp edges and tightly wound threads.

The more certain I was that I loved him.

Breathing the words aloud was the simplest thing—so simple I forgot to feel anxious. "I love you."

He pulled back just far enough to meet my eyes. His voice was velvety and warm, and only for my ears as he said, "I love you too."

The most natural thing in the world.

Need more wintery goodness reads?! Check out Just Fake Married

Two lies and a fake marriage later...

Veterinarian Owen could blame being shy, but telling a donor at the dog shelter he works at that he's married was... a mistake. Now, he has to figure out how to get out of the lie. And it doesn't help that he also told Emmeline, the woman he can't stop thinking about, the whole misguided tale.

Emmeline can't believe Owen, possibly the hottest man alive, lied about his marital status, but then when her client refuses to work with an unmarried woman, she did the exact same thing. She's desperate to keep her falsehood quiet as she figures out how to not become the saleswoman *who made up a husband* in her very male-dominated field.

When Emmeline's and Owen's worlds unexpectedly collide, they need to double down on their stories or watch them explode in their faces.

As the deception grows so does their attraction, but can their relationship survive under the weight of so many lies?
https://books2read.com/u/m2Edk1

Hazel and Elijah Don't Get Caught

Grand Ridge is for Lovers Prequel

Hazel

Everyonein Grand Ridge, Michigan knew Elijah March. He'd been a senior when I'd been a sophomore. Having a crush on him had been almost a rite of passage for people my age. *Oh, you graduated between 2010 and 2015? What was your Elijah March phase?*

Mine? I'd signed up for all of them.

Baseball Elijah? Yeah, he wasn't our star player, but he was the only reason I showed up to games.

Golden-boy Elijah? Yes, please, he had a smile that could charm anyone. It was never directed at me—a nerdy younger girl with frizzy brown hair—but I was still charmed by it.

Rebellious Elijah? Oh, hell yes. He still had the smile, and played baseball, but with a little extra "Fuck You" on his shoulder. He skipped school to do… whatever kids who skip school do; I was never one of them. And he joined the other rebels to drink in Ol' Mr. Miller's backwoods—or so I heard.

His major rebellion, though, was sleeping around; rumor around school said he was *very* good at it. Again, I wouldn't know because I didn't have sex in high school, good *or* bad.

But I *was* late to class once because Sarah Hillis was telling Olivia Vazquez salacious details about him. In my, and their defense, the girls hadn't realized I was in a bathroom stall. It would have been too awkward to leave, so I waited until they had gone. It was worth it for the details I inadvertently discovered.

The rebellious stage was right around the time his mom left his dad, and the church-going, God-fearing community had certainly had opinions on the matter. After Elijah graduated, he and his mom moved to Nashville—or Memphis; I wasn't sure—he'd been estranged from his dad ever since.

I only knew the last part because his dad was my mentor; Dr. March, our town's veterinarian.

When he talked to me that morning to say Elijah was visiting and planned to help us later, I was curious, but not overly invested. I wasn't the fawning, nerdy girl with an unrequited crush from ten years ago. I was now a nerdy woman a month away from taking over Dr. March's vet clinic.

My vet clinic. Almost.

I was too busy and overwhelmed to pay much attention to handsome—or not handsome—men.

It made Dr. March's next warning unnecessary. "You need to stay away from Elijah. He'd be bad for your reputation."

I blinked, completely caught off guard. "My reputation? I don't think we need to worry about that."

"He will try to take advantage of you."

"Why would you say that?" The corners of my mouth turned down.

Dr.March shook his head. "I know my son."

"Noone is going to take advantage of me—"

"Hazel, stay away from him," he said with a razor-sharp edge to his voice. "My son has a history, and it would be unwise to ignore it. If you get involved with him, it could affect the sale of the clinic."

"How?" I'd seen the ownership documents; Elijah March wasn't insinuated anywhere on them.

Dr. March's face grew red, and his jaw set. "Do as I ask, please."

By the time evening rolled around, I'd mulled over the conversation. It was still on my mind as I put on a summer dress that ended at my ankles and fit like a T-shirt. The perfect outfit to prep for our annual pet adoption event on the local library's side yard.

The sun was setting when I parked my vehicle next to the historical, large-stone building. There were a few patrons inside, but I was the first from the clinic to arrive. A half hour later, Nora, our business administrator, and Dr. Marchwere directing our other two veterinarians, Brooks and Remi, as they lined up the temporary fencing on the side yard.

Car tires crunched over loose stones on the paved parking lot, catching my attention. The car was black and sleek, but not overly sporty. Through the windshield, I could make out that it was a man driving.

Then he stepped out into the summer evening, and I swear by all things I know to be true, time slowed down. It was like a scene out of an early aughts romantic comedy, with the warm breeze rustling through his chestnut-colored curls and a beautiful smile underneath dark sunglasses.

Completely absorbed in the way his gray T-shirt draped over his shoulders and chest, I lost track of my slack-jawed expression. Until Nora turned to share a wide-eyed look.

This was Elijah March all grown up.

He made polite introductions, not even sparing me a lingering glance—which was fine. Really.

He helped us prepare, diligently working while making conversation. The whole time, he and I orbited—but never entered—each other's space. That didn't stop me from noticing the way the fine muscles in his forearm flexed as he painted the welcome sign, or the bulge of his biceps as he hammered the temporary fenceposts into their bases. Or just the general way his thighs filled out his jeans.

My gaze seemed to land on him, no matter what I was *supposed* to be focused on.

By the time we finished, Nora and I had had a silent chat with eyebrow raises,suppressed smirks, and pointed staring—more or less meaning, *Are you seeing how hot he is?*

We really needed to actually talk.

Elijah said goodbye and left. Shortly after Nora and I were in our separate cars, and before I'd even put my car in drive, I dialed her.

"How is your heart doing?" she asked through the speaker.

"Palpitations. Did you see that man?" I answered, my voice pitched high.

She snorted. "Yeah. Got a whole eye full."

"Shoot. What do I gotta do to get more eyes on him?"

"Such an important question, and I don't have an answer. But did you see how weird Doc was with him?"

"He was weird earlier today, too, when he was talking about Elijah coming tonight."

The conversation weaved through different degrees of "he was really polite," and "it was nice of him to help out," and "he is so hot," until I parked in front of the clinic. I had a few things I needed to grab for tomorrow's event.

I pushed my key into the door with my phone pressed to my ear.

"So,is this an official reentry into 'I want to marry Elijah March' town?" Nora asked.

"One hundred percent." My voice carried across the empty lobby and the front office. "What the fuck was evolution thinking when it made him so goddamn fine?"

Her smile was clear through the phone. "Superfluously good look-ing."

"Like,I get it, I want him to impregnate me. You don't have to keep making such a point of it."

"Yeah,every angle of that man had something new to appreciate."

"Goddamngorgeous." I pushed through the door to the hallway lined with exam rooms on the right. Taking a left, I entered the office, heading to the files at the back of the room. "I thought I'd outgrown my 'Elijah March Scrambles my Brain' phase, but I have not."

"Ido what?" a deep male voice said from behind me.

I made a sound somewhere between a gasp and a scream, turning around so quickly I pushed a couple files off the shelf. They slapped onto the thin blue carpet. My hand pressed to my chest.

In my ear, Nora sounded worried. "What's going on? Are you okay?"

Elijah sat back in a black office chair. One of his ankles was propped on the thigh of his other leg. The cotton of his shirt draped and stretched across his chest in the most delicious ways. His chin rested on his fist. The fingers of his other hand relaxed over the armrest. His hair was ruffled, the curls flipped in all directions. A hint of a smile flirted with his lips.

His green eyes focused on only me—interested and playful.

My mouth hung open. A warm blush filled my cheeks. I should say *something*, but my thoughts had gone to ground like a scared animal; abandoning me to static between my ears.

"Tellme you're okay. Fuck. I'm coming to you," Nora's voice continued through the speaker. It took me a second to comprehend her words.

"I'm fine. Sorry, I'm okay. You don't have to come here." My calm tone was a total lie.

"Are you sure?"

"Yeah,Elijah March is here."

"No!" Nora drew out the word, loud enough that Elijah raised an eyebrow.

I continued my fake facade. "Yup, I was just startled."

"Ohmygod! No."

"Mm-hm, I'll talk to you later." I ended the call.

"Sorry to startle you," Elijah rumbled.

I was too mortified to appreciate the rich timbre of his voice, which was a shame. "No need to apologize. What are you doing here?"

"Helping my dad with something; he let me in. I'm just waiting."

I decided ignoring that he'd heard me was the best way forward. "Your car at the back of the building?"

"Yeah,that's why you didn't see it."

"Great.Well, I'll leave you be."

I was fully ready to disappear into my office and wish for death, but he said, "You think evolution went too far with me?"

With my back to him, I allowed myself a momentary cringe.

"I'm sorry?" My face was neutral when I turned around.

"That's what you said."

I remember.

"You heard that?"

"Yeah, you might not recall because I scramble your brain?"

"No need to rehash the past."

"Why not?"

"Because I'm flustered." Embarrassed would be more accurate. Humiliated. Where was the hole I could hide in?

"I'm a little flustered, too."

I grimaced. "Oh yeah, you seem it."

"I'm just better at hiding it than you."

"Hm."

He tilted his head, considering me. "We had a biology class together, didn't we?"

"I think so."

Definitely.

"You raised your hand a lot."

"Good of you to remember."

"You were cute."

"Yeah, I'm sure."

"You're still cute."

Was Elijah March flirting with me? How was I supposed to respond to this? It'd been so long since anyone had shown interest in me that I was out of practice. But despite having built him up in my memory, he was just a man. And I was a grown woman.

There was no reasonable reason for me to feel like I was melting.

"Thank you," I said to my ballerina flats. My hands clasped against my thighs. My shoulders shrugged forward, as if I could hide standing right there. My body language made me recall my wallflower days before I'd gone to college and had come into my confidence. It was enough to convince me to roll my shoulders back, straighten my spine, and lift my chin. "I think you're cute."

Oh my god, I wanted to swallow my tongue. I'd flown too close to the sun. How had I thought I could go from him hearing my gossiping to telling him he was cute without it being weird?

A slow, easy smile spread across his face, and the full force of it was overwhelmingly charming. I'd never been so charmed in my life. I would die a charmed woman.

Elijah met my eye. "I was told you're a good girl."

My jaw dropped, his words filthy and enticing.

The pink tip of his tongue moistened his lips. "Are you a good girl?"

I had to swallow to answer. "Usually." Air rushed from my lungs as the lie settled into my blood, and I corrected, "Fucking *always*."

I had always been *such* a good girl. So mature for my age. So driven and focused. And I'd never wanted to be anything else. I liked being good, dependable. In my twenty-six years, I'd never put my foot out of line. But right now Elijah was making me want to be anything but good.To ignore the warning—possible threat—his dad had given, and experience something I'd always wanted but thought I could never have.

Theway Elijah's gaze swept over my body made me think I could have everything.

He gripped the arms of the chair. "I was told to keep my distance."

A flair of irritation shot through me—knowing exactly who had overstepped their boundaries. Dr. March and I would be having a conversation about him staying in his lane.

I raised my chin. "I don't remember telling you that."

Elijah's eyebrows shot up, and he nodded. "That's a good point. That's a *good* fucking point."

He stood in one graceful movement. "Is this too close?"

I rolled my eyes, but the effect was ruined by the giant grin on my face. "No."

He took a step closer, only a few feet away now. Close enough that I could smell faint wisps of something smoky and sweet. "Is this too close?"

"No."

Was this really happening?

He reached for me, slowly. Softly, he asked, "Is this too close?"

His fingertips slipped up my hips to my waist. My chest felt tight. My heart was racing. My mind could only process so much information over the flurry of electricity shocking through my nervous system. There was a darkening of stubble on his jaw. One peak of his Cupid's bow was slightly sharper than the other. In his eyes was the question he'd asked.

"No," I breathed.

A shiver ran down my spine as he slipped his hands around to my back. Instead of moving closer to me, he pulled me into him. My breasts pressed to his chest. I took hold of his arms, just because I could—just because I wanted to. The firm contours of muscles were even better under my touch than I'd imagined.

He tilted his head, his lips parted inches from mine.

"It's not close enough," I answered before he could ask.

Swallowing, he nodded. "Yeah."

One of his palms moved up my back to cup my neck at my pulse. His thumb drew a line along my jaw. "Your heart's beating fast."

"Mm-hm," was all I could actually say.

"Are you sure you're okay? Do you feel safe?"

His question caught me off guard, and I instinctively searched for the answer. He was wrapped around me, firm and strong. Real. So much more than a fantasy.

"I do." I sank into him, noticing the way his heart thrummed against his chest.

"Good."

"Do you feel safe?"

He blinked. His hold on me tightened. The corner of his mouth curved as he lowered his head to brush his lips along my earlobe. I gasped as intense sensations flickered through my body.

I felt more than heard him groan. "Yes."

I'd never done this. He wasn't a stranger, but he nearly was. Everything about this fought against my logical mind, but even my logical self said, *Don't question it.*

Against my thigh, his cock twitched.

Heat pooled in my core—a throbbing need.

My eyelids drifted shut as he skimmed his lips along my jaw; turning me to liquid.Bewitched by the gentle caress of his touch. Anticipation coiled in my stomach,waiting as the pressure grew. The corner of his mouth brushed mine. I turned my head, ready for real contact.

The back door closed with a loud thud. We jumped apart as if we'd been splashed with cold water. The spell was broken. My head whipped in the direction of foot steps coming closer down the hallway.

Elijah ran a hand through his hair, his fingers tangling in the curls. One corner of his mouth turned up in an apologetic and bashful smile. "Fuck, sorry. You're..."

I leaned forward to hear his quiet words.

"You're really fucking beautiful."

Nothing was working like it should—my jaw was slack, my hands hung at my sides, and if not for the shelf behind me, I probably would have fallen to the floor.

Ata normal volume, he said, "It was nice to talk to you." Then, without any more explanation, he left the office. "Hey, Dad."

"Hazel in there?" Dr. March asked.

"Yeah."

I bent to pick up the files that had fallen when I'd come in, and placed them back on the shelf where they belonged. Dr. March stepped into the room, and I hoped my voice was as level as Elijah's had been. "I swung by to grab some adoption applications."

"Well,good thing you remembered." He looked from me to Elijah, who was standing in the doorway, but I wasn't sure what he was looking for. Whatever it was, I hoped he didn't find it.

"Of course." My expression felt natural enough, possibly a bit forced. "Anyway, Iwon't hold you two up. It was nice to catch up with you, Elijah."

"You,too."

I tossed a wave over my shoulder and found Elijah watching me leave. Even from the other side of the lobby, I could feel the intensity of his stare. A regret of what had almost passed between us. A promise for more.

The past few minutes didn't feel real. It was already a hazy memory of bright emotions and awareness.

But I knew without a doubt that I wanted it to happen again.

Keep reading for free! https://dl.bookfunnel.com/c2xuxoo5f7

Acknowledgements

This book never wanted to be completed. Not that it didn't want to be written, it just didn't want me to put my focus anywhere else. It was supposed to be a short story, then a short novella, and now it's nearly a short novel. So, trust the process, I guess.

Thank you to my husband and kids. Your support is invaluable. You're my whole heart.

Through all the ups and downs, my lovely Smut Coven has had my back. I don't know how I would write books without them.

A big thank you to Heather with Simply Spellbound Edits. All of your *lol's* and suggestions were equally helpful! You're the best!

To Kate Prior, my amazing cover artist, thank you! You are also my number one story fixer. Talking about story with you are some of my favorite conversations. Ever. I'm so grateful that you're my friend. I love you!

Nell Sandpaper!!! You have been cheerleading this book, and it has motivated me to keep going. To try harder. To let the book be what it needed to be. I hope you love it, you beautiful sunflower.

To my incredible advance readers and fans! Friends, your reviews and excitement mean the world to me! I love writing these cozy rom-coms, I'm ecstatic for every single one of my fans. I feel so lucky. Thank you.

What would my acknowledgements be without recognizing my mom? No matter what I do, you think I'm the best at it. I can't tell you how much I appreciate it.

ABOUT MARTY

Marty Vee is the midwestern gal who is going to banter her steamy contemporary small town into only one bed, time after time. The friends will become lovers, and so will the enemies.

She lives in the Mitten State with her introverted husband, two feral children, the fluffiest house cat, and her tender-hearted rescue dog.

She loves singing (constantly) and meandering hikes through the woods.

Learn more about her other books at www.martyvee.com

Find her on Instagram @martyveeauthor

www.ingramcontent.com/pod-product-compliance
Lightning Source LLC
Chambersburg PA
CBHW060447300726

48975CB00008B/2422